CHOCOLATE MAGIC

Other books by Zelda Benjamin:

The *Love by Chocolate* Romance series:

Chocolate Secrets

Brooklyn Ballerina

CHOCOLATE MAGIC

•

Zelda Benjamin

AVALON BOOKS
NEW YORK

Published by Thomas Bouregy & Co., Inc.
160 Madison Avenue, New York, NY 10016

Library of Congress Cataloging-in-Publication Data

Benjamin, Zelda.
  Chocolate magic / Zelda Benjamin.
        p. cm. — (The love by chocolate romance series)
    ISBN 978-0-8034-7752-0 (hardcover : acid-free paper)
    1. Chocolate—Fiction.   2. Inheritance and succession—
Fiction.   3. Specialty stores—Fiction.   4. Brooklyn
(New York, N.Y.)—Fiction.   I. Title.
    PS3602.E664C45 2010
    813'.6—dc22

                                                    2009045030

PRINTED IN THE UNITED STATES OF AMERICA
ON ACID-FREE PAPER
BY HADDON CRAFTSMEN, BLOOMSBURG, PENNSYLVANIA

Eating chocolate is always more fun when shared with people you care about.

I would like to thank my critique partners, Allison Chase, Nancy Cohen, Sharon Hartley, Karen Kendall, and Cynthia Thomason for sharing the chocolate experience.

My husband, Ben, and my children, Melissa and Michael, and my grandchildren, Jesse and Zoey, who willingly offered to help out with all the chocolate tasting and research. What a hard job!

Then there are the wonderful chocolate shops I visited—Chocolate Garden in New York, NY, and Schoc Chocolate in Wellington, New Zealand.

Chapter One

A giant hot dog ran down Union Street calling Chloe Brandeau's name.

Chloe prayed it was a figment of her imagination, a delusion brought on by sleep deprivation. No such luck. The giant hot dog wobbled closer.

With no means of escape, she backed up against the door of her chocolate shop. Henry, last night's blind date, had taken her a little too seriously when she had suggested, *If you're ever in the neighborhood, stop by.*

Chloe turned toward the door, hoping that when she glanced back, the huge weiner would be gone. What had happened to her boringly predictable life?

Henry's appearance was not the only unusual

1

occurrence this morning. Jogging six blocks from the Butler Street apartment building she had recently inherited to her chocolate shop on Union Street was not part of her normal morning routine. Her late start was attributed to a group of hysterical tenants pounding on her door at 2:00 A.M.—or had it been 3:00?

Did it really matter what time the tenant in apartment 2C had frantically rung her doorbell? Mr. Liang in apartment 3C had left his water running again. Water from his bathtub had cascaded down the walls into the apartment below, threatening to ruin Sadie Katz's precious stuffed bulldog collection.

Chloe's body ached, and her breaths came short and quick. Her face felt flushed. She imagined that her cheeks were as bright pink as the frosted tips of her spiked hair.

This morning's combined events were enough to make a girl want to drown in chocolate: Sadie, Mr Liang, and now Henry, all before 9:00 A.M.

"Hi, Chloe. It's me, Henry." The giant hot dog wiggled to a stop just short of her toes.

Chloe forced a smile. Unsure how to greet a man dressed in culinary drag, she managed a weak, "Hi, Henry."

Under that awful costume, Henry, a short, chubby, bald man, was nice enough but definitely not her type. She took pity on him. After all, it wasn't his fault that Chloe had let her friend Sarah convince her to go on the date. Hoping to avoid an awkward situation, Chloe had said good night in his car and foolishly told Henry to stop by her shop anytime. She never imagined he would show up. And certainly not the next morning.

Here he was, fuzzy, plush, and smelling like one of Sadie's wet bulldogs. A twinge of pity returned. Poor man, stuffed inside such an obnoxious costume on this unusually warm April morning. But that's where her compassion for the man started and ended.

Chloe pushed her smile up a notch. "Thanks for stopping by, Henry. You really should get back to your post." She turned the key and pushed on the door, anxious to escape into the security of her shop. The rows of dark chocolate truffles and happy pecan turtles would easily help her forget the way her day had started.

Too late. People on the street stopped and stared. The giant hot dog attracted smirks and chuckles. This couldn't be good for Chloe's business. She created and sold fine handmade chocolates. An oversized hot dog in front of her shop was not the kind of advertising she wanted.

Henry took advantage of the attention and passed out his putrid green flyers. Chloe stepped away and answered her cell phone.

"Hi, Chloe. How'd your date go?" Sarah, Chloe's self-appointed matchmaker, who was responsible for this whole sticky situation, sounded much too cheerful.

"Wait until I get my hands on you," Chloe whispered.

"Something wrong?"

"Henry's here," Chloe answered through gritted teeth.

"Great. I knew the two of you had a lot in common, both of you being in the food industry."

"No. It's not great. And I don't consider dressing as a giant hot dog comparable to 'being in the food industry.' " Chloe released a slow, exasperated breath. "Your matchmaking contract is terminated, my friend."

"Food snob," Sarah laughed. "You're not getting off so easily. You agreed to give me three chances to find you the right man. Don't you want to take a date to the Chocolate Ball? You can't back out now, after only one date."

"Oh, yes I can. I don't need a dating consultant." Chloe knew Sarah had a valid argument. A date for the ball would be nice, but that was weeks away. Henry was here now, and she couldn't chance any more dates like this. "Just stick to your accounting. You're much better at handling my money than you are at finding me a date."

"What money? Have you forgotten how low your bank account has gotten since you inherited the money pit from your late aunt?"

"Things will turn around."

"I hope so. But would it be so terrible if I found you a nice man with a decent paycheck?" Sarah believed a date with the right man could solve even Chloe's disastrous financial situation.

"Money isn't everything." Chloe's grip tightened around her phone. Usually its sparkling bling decorations made her smile, but not today. "I don't have time for this."

"Yes, you do." Sarah insisted. "You can't spend your life making chocolate for other people's sweethearts and never have time to find your own true love."

"My own true love." Chloe forced a harsh laugh. Her life *was* limited to her chocolate. The Chocolate Boutique was her boyfriend and her social life. "I doubt he exists." She watched Henry hand out his flyers. If she decided to let Sarah complete their agreement, Chloe needed to believe that her dates couldn't get any worse than Henry.

"C'mon. Give me two more chances. I promise—"

"Okay, but I'm only doing this so you'll leave me alone. I've got to go. He's coming back." Chloe shuddered. She was reluctant to agree to Sarah's plan. She didn't need a man to support her. She had been doing just fine on her own until her Aunt Bessie's building had started caving in around her.

She would think of something. She never compromised when making her candies. She wasn't about to lower her standards to find a way out of her temporary financial predicament either. But an occasional date might help take her mind off the situation.

At the moment, though, the problem was not her lack of a social life or even her late Aunt Bessie's apartment building. The source of her distress was Henry. He had to be sent on his way as quickly as possible.

"Henry, you'll miss the morning rush-hour crowd if you hang around here. Smith Street is a much better location for you." With her hand on his back to steady him, Chloe grabbed one side of the plush bun, turning him in the direction he had just come from.

He was reluctant to move. Only when she gently nudged him did he finally inch forward. At the curb he stopped. A high-priced black SUV pulled into the loading zone, blocking him from crossing the street.

Henry pointed to the sign over his head. "Hey, you can't park here."

Chloe knew the car was not making a delivery. She had seen that vehicle several times before, and each time whoever stepped out of the car brought nothing but trouble.

Ever since the reading of her aunt's will, an anonymous buyer had sent his agents with offers to buy Chloe's run-down apartment building. They all arrived in the same ominous SUV carrying briefcases full of papers with lucrative offers. Each one used a different tactic, trying to persuade Chloe to sign on the dotted line.

Tempting as the money was, Chloe wouldn't sell. She couldn't. Not only had she made a promise to her aunt, but the building had become her home.

She waited at the curb to see whom the mysterious buyer had sent today. She hoped it wasn't the little accountant wearing baggy pants who always chose a sample of her most expensive chocolate. And she could handle the tough-looking attorney who, after a magical sip of her hot cocoa, softened like a melted candy kiss.

Dark tinted windows made it difficult to see into the backseat. She tried to stare past her reflection, but the feeling that someone in there was watching her made her look away. She stepped back beside Henry and waited. The driver, who usually waited in the car, stepped out to open the back door.

Definitely someone important has come today. She didn't care who was in the car. They couldn't park in her loading zone. She started to tell the driver to move the vehicle, when a man stepped from the backseat onto the curb. She recognized him immediately from his picture on the cover of this week's issue of *Financial Times.*

Ethan Behar, a self-made millionaire, had looked pleasant enough on the magazine cover, but standing here in front of her, he was drop-dead gorgeous.

She didn't want to like anything about him and searched for a flaw. This man, a master of acquisitions, was after her Aunt Bessie's apartment building. He might be considered attractive, if she'd liked his style, but he was much too conservative in his tailor-made suit to be her type. In spite of his well-made clothes, she noticed his rugged good looks. His commanding features suggested not only physical strength but also the kind of determination seen in self-made men.

Chloe prided herself on her ability to read people. That talent helped her sell the right chocolates to the right customers and bring them back for more. She felt a strange sadness. Her inner vibes told her that this man, a victim of his own success, had no time to indulge in such a trivial luxury as chocolate.

Next to her, Henry shifted impatiently. Ethan Behar casually glanced at the giant hot dog. His lopsided smile suggested he was only slightly amused. Dismissing Henry, he turned his attention to Chloe. An unexpected attraction jolted her. The uneasy and unwelcome feeling made her turn away from his gaze. She looked down at her jeweled shoes from the six-dollar table at a local yard sale.

Behar stepped closer. She couldn't help but notice his expensive leather loafers against the cracked sidewalk. Her eyes moved upward. It was difficult to ignore the sensuality of the man's well-toned body. She stopped at his eyes. He studied her too, only he seemed more comfortable.

Men like this had Wharton MBAs and more tactics up their sleeves than there were stripes on a candy cane. They did not look twice at girls like her, a graduate of Ecole du Chocolat with hair tips frosted to match the season.

When he finally spoke, there was a slight tinge of surprise in his voice. "You must be Chloe Brandeau." He extended his hand. "I'm Ethan Behar."

His presence made her uneasy. She knew why he was here, but she wasn't rude. She placed her hand in his. "I know who you are."

With the gentrification of this Brooklyn neighborhood, it wasn't unusual to see celebrities or almost celebrities on the streets or in her shop. She was not the type to be awestruck or intimidated by fame or fortune. She intended to let Mr. Behar know from the beginning that his notoriety did not impress her.

"It's nice of you to show up in person instead of sending one of your hired guns to do your bidding." Chloe felt no need to sugarcoat her words. She had chocolate bunny orders to fill for the upcoming holiday and was already behind schedule. She placed her hands on her hips and added, "You're wasting your precious time."

"Wasting my time?"

"Yes. I read all about you in the *Financial Times.* Should I remind you what the article said?" She proceeded to quote verbatim the writer's words. "There aren't enough hours in the day for a man like Ethan Behar."

"You read the *Financial Times*?" He raised an eyebrow and studied her as if they were alone on the street. He hesitated a moment before asking, "What'd you think of the interview?"

Caught off guard by the seriousness of his question, she responded with a short but true answer. "It was informative. You're a very determined man." She wasn't about to admit that she had been impressed by his common-sense approach to business. Other articles she had read referred to his street-smarts as Emotional Intelligence. She gathered from the article that Ethan Behar had no time for such foolish labels either.

"Do you always believe everything you read?" he asked. His inquiry sounded more like a challenge than a question.

"Of course not." Chloe warned herself not to take the bait. She shifted her weight, unsure if he was impressed that she had actually read the article or with his own replies to the interviewer's questions.

"Neither do I. That's why I'm here. The reports on my desk stated you were difficult." His eyes drifted to her face. "I had to see for myself if what my 'hired guns' wrote was true."

She lifted her shoulders, hoping she looked authoritative in spite of her colorful appearance. "Your interview stated you meet every new experience with a firm yet flexible attitude." She tried to contain her curtness. "Should I believe that?"

"Touché." His bemused smile hinted that he was enjoying her confrontation.

"It's obvious you're not showing any flexibility and don't seem to understand that my building is not for sale." It was too late to worry that he would realize she had taken such a strong interest in his interview. "Mr. Behar, even now that I know you're the interested buyer, nothing has changed. My building is not for sale." There was no reason to beat around the bush now that the master of acquisitions stood face-to-face with her.

A gentle spring breeze rustled the hem of her vintage Chanel skirt, exposing more of her leg than she cared to show.

The view did not go unnoticed. Ethan's glance slid to her bare leg. He scanned her from her legs to the spiked pink points of her hair. "Interesting hairdo."

Chloe's face, still flushed from her morning jog, couldn't get any redder. If his comment was a ploy to soften her up before he came in for the kill, she wasn't falling for it. "The color is in anticipation of the coming of spring."

"Interesting sales tactic." He glanced briefly to her

right, dismissing Henry with a look of uncertainty. "What's the power you have to send my representatives back without ever discussing business?" His gray eyes softened. "Was it you or your chocolate?"

"You're more than welcome to stop into my shop and try a sample."

"I'm not as easily distracted as my agents." His tone was smooth with an edge of steel that sent a shiver down her spine. His dark eyebrow arched mischievously. "I just might stop in and sample some of that charm I heard so much about."

"I'm only offering chocolate."

Her life could be a lot easier if she forgot her promise to her aunt and accepted Ethan Behar's offer. All her energy and money could be concentrated on her shop. She could take a vacation—go to Belgium and study new chocolate-making techniques. With a shake of her head she banished the thought. If she sold, who would care about Mrs. Katz's bulldogs, Mr. Liang, or the other tenants in Aunt Bessie's building?

"Did you at least listen to their offers while you seduced my men?"

"Where's your famous flexibility? You're not listening to what I'm saying. The building is not for sale." Trying not to sound too curt, she added, "There's nothing else for us to discuss."

Chloe had forgotten that Henry was still there but was quickly reminded when he joined the conversation. "Hey, I read all about you in the paper. You just bought the old ironworks building on Butler Street. It's part of a plan to build some kind of condo complex." Henry might not be the spiciest hot dog in the bunch, but he had something to offer. "Oops." He turned to Chloe. "You live on Butler Street."

Chloe drew an uneven breath. She did a quick calculation. Her building stood only a few doors away from the recently sold ironworks. The sale had meant nothing to her until this moment. Now everything began to make sense.

"And you are . . . ?" Ethan looked at Henry from the corner of his eye.

"This is Henry. He's a . . ." Chloe searched for a word to explain their association and, for lack of anything better, said, "He's a friend. He's going back to work."

"I am?" A disappointed Henry turned to leave.

Ethan's driver opened the door before Chloe had a chance to shout a warning. The door clipped Henry's bun, and he spun around like meat on a rotisserie. The top-heavy costume caught him off balance, and he toppled to the sidewalk. Squirming, he made a vain attempt to get up.

"Oh, Henry, are you okay?" Chloe kneeled beside him, unsure what to do.

People stopped and laughed. Ladies from the beauty shop next door congregated at the window. Again

Henry had managed to create a scene, but this time it wasn't his fault.

Chloe winced at the pained look on Henry's face as he rubbed the back of his head.

"I'm bleeding." Henry held up his hand, his fingers as red as ketchup.

"You bumped your head." She wanted to shout at him that this never would have happened if he hadn't come wobbling over. "Don't worry. Head wounds always bleed a lot." She looked up and glared at Ethan. "This is all your fault."

"Let me help." Ethan stood over them and extended his hand to Chloe. With the other hand he pointed to the group of foil-haired ladies congregated at the window of the beauty shop. "I'd hate for you to be the object of their morning gossip." He reached into his pocket and handed Henry a monogrammed handkerchief. "My driver, Brad, and I will get him onto his feet." An edge of annoyance chilled his voice.

Did the infamous Mr. Behar dislike a scene? The damage was already done. The neighborhood busybodies had cell phones to their ears.

Chloe knew firsthand how juicy local gossip traveled like wildfire. When she started out as an employee at the Chocolate Boutique five years ago, no one had seemed to care much about a funky twenty-five-year-old with a talent for creating irresistible chocolate. Even when old

Max Martinelli retired and left her half ownership of the shop, no one cared a chocolate lick.

However, when Aunt Bessie died and left the Butler Street apartment building to Chloe instead of her son, Allen, the big-shot attorney, everyone in the neighborhood had an opinion. But Chloe couldn't care less what they had to say as long as they bought her chocolate.

Ethan impressed her with his take-charge attitude and concern for her reputation. He easily could have gotten into his vehicle and driven away, leaving her with the consequences of a bleeding hot dog in front of her store. Still, independent and self-sufficient, Chloe preferred to do things herself. She saw no need to feel obligated to a man, especially a man like Ethan.

She made one more attempt to get Henry onto his feet. Hard as she tried, she couldn't stand him up. Reluctantly she placed her hand in Ethan's. His grip was strong, and he assisted her to her feet with little effort.

"You're light as a feather." He pulled her close to his chest. He emitted a sense of male strength, a sharp contrast to poor Henry, lying at their feet. "Don't you eat any of those candies you sell?"

"Eat my profit margin?" Chloe retorted, and she stepped back.

"You not only read *Financial Times,* you also speak my language." He appraised her with a calculating glance. "I may have underestimated the effort I have to put into this acquisition."

She took a deep breath. His voice, strong, sensual, and complimentary, had suddenly upset her balance. "You never lose, do you?"

"Why get into a game you don't intend to win?" He handed his jacket to his driver. "Brad, give me a hand, and let's get this guy up on his feet." Together they turned Henry upright. Blood trickled around his ear. "Call an ambulance." Ethan tossed Brad his Black-Berry.

"No ambulance, no hospital," Henry protested. "I don't have insurance." He started to walk away. His gait was unsteady, and Ethan rushed forward to support him.

Chloe's attention should have been on poor Henry, but she couldn't take her eyes off Ethan and the perfect fit of his crisp blue shirt, another tailor-made garment. She would bet the price of that shirt could pay a plumber to fix her leaky pipes.

More people had gathered around Henry, filling the sidewalk in front of her shop. It was hard to ignore their snickers and smirks as Ethan and his driver stuffed a reluctant Henry, bun and all, into the SUV.

"Where are you taking Henry?" Chloe asked.

"We'll take him to the hospital." Ethan slammed the back door, catching the tip of the hot dog.

Chloe winced, expecting Henry to scream out in pain. A quick reality check reminded her that Henry was not an actual hot dog. "You can't just take him away."

"He needs to see a doctor. Looks like he needs some stitches on the back of his head." Ethan opened the door, releasing the fuzzy fabric, then slammed it shut again. He glanced in the window and gave Henry a thumbs-up before climbing into the front passenger seat.

Chloe ran around to the front of the car and banged on the window. "He has no insurance!" she shouted.

Ethan rolled down the window and said, "Don't worry, I'll cover the bill." He didn't seem at all put out by the sudden change in his plans.

"You'll let me know how he is?" Chloe asked, "won't you?" She reached into her pocket and handed him a business card.

Ethan glanced at the card and smiled. "I've already got your number. I'll be back to take care of our unfinished business."

Chapter Two

Chloe stood at the curb longer than necessary and watched the SUV until it was out of sight. Her day was so out of sync, she hoped that once she entered her shop, the power of the chocolate would set everything straight.

Inside her shop she stopped and inhaled the sweet, nutty scent, but nothing happened. She exhaled slowly, took another breath, and waited for the familiar feeling of serenity. But her body still felt tense and out of tune from the events of the morning. She stepped behind the counter, walked to the sink, and ran her hands under warm water. Massaging creamy, chocolate-scented soap into her palms, she let her mind drift. Images of

Ethan stepping out of his car, approaching her, and driving away with Henry were embedded in her brain.

She dried her hands and walked to the counter. She removed a tray of chocolate turtles and started to rearrange them, placing the fuller ones toward the front. Several minutes of the mindless task and her thoughts were back where they should be—on selling chocolate.

Her mood had changed just in time for the first customer of the day. She looked up and saw one of the foil-haired, beauty parlor ladies enter.

But today, Ida, a regular customer, did not have chocolate on her mind. "Is it true Ethan Behar wants to buy all the stores on the block?"

Chloe shook her head, speechless, amazed at how quickly rumors started.

"You're not selling?" Ida approached the counter.

Ida did not elaborate on what Chloe was not selling. Was she referring to her Union Street shop or her Butler Street apartment building?

"No, I'm not selling. Nothing I own is for sale, especially to Ethan Behar." If she ever thought of selling, it would never be to someone who considered this all some kind of high-stakes game he had no intention of losing.

Chloe pulled another tray of candy from the showcase. She stared at the alternating rows of dark, milk, and white chocolates. The arrangement attracted Ida's attention.

"Do you have any of those delicious raspberry-filled truffles?"

Chloe reached for a square of white paper and took a truffle from the display case. She hoped chewing would keep Ida quiet.

No such luck. "What was Henry doing here this morning?" Ida asked between nibbles of chocolate. "His mother and I are old friends." Ida might be nosy, but she knew how to eat fine chocolate. She took small, delicate bites, savoring the flavor with each nibble.

"I never met Henry's mother, and I just met Henry last night." It made Chloe feel good to watch Ida enjoy her candy.

"This is delicious. I'll take a quarter pound." Ida wiped her lips. She leaned across the counter and whispered, "I heard all about your deal with Sarah, the matchmaker. It's about time you think of something other than chocolate."

"Sarah is not a matchmaker. She's my accountant and likes to play around at matchmaking." It was unlike her friend not to be discreet. Ida must have talked to Henry's mother. These beauty-parlor ladies could never keep anything under their hair-dryer bonnets. Chloe braced herself for what was coming next.

"Matchmaker, dating consultant, beautician,

hairdresser . . ." Ida waved her fingers in the air. "They're all the same—just depends on which generation you're talking to. What they do doesn't change." Ida pointed to Chloe's signature chocolate and asked. "How much are those?"

"Twenty-one dollars a pound."

"Too pricey for me. I'll take a quarter pound of the chocolate-covered orange slices too."

Chloe weighed out a quarter pound of fruit and tossed a dark-chocolate–covered ganache into the bag. She wanted Ida out. "This one's on the house."

"You're so sweet. You know, if Sarah can't find you the man of your dreams, I know some nice single men." Ida handed Chloe a ten-dollar bill.

Chloe fumbled with the change. She knew Ida would share not only her chocolates with the beauty parlor ladies, but also the news that Chloe had signed on with a matchmaker. She imagined the onslaught of speculation as to why she'd agreed to such a plan. Soon every aunt, mother, and grandmother would come into her shop and pretend they were interested in buying her chocolate. They would all manage to drop the name of some young relative they thought would be her perfect match.

She shuddered at the idea of meeting more Henry the Hot Dogs. The only good side was, she would sell more candy.

Unwanted suitors should be easy enough to distract.

She'd serve them chocolate and delude them the same way she had Ethan Behar's henchmen. She always kept a close watch on the latest chocolate research. Unlike women, men craved pizza first, with chocolate close behind. She had thoughts about presenting a chocolate pizza as her entry at the upcoming Chocolate Ball. With its panel of male judges, her pizza could be a strong competitor.

She turned and looked at the wall lined with ancient Mayan tools. All of them had been used in chocolate rituals. They were artifacts believed to have magical powers, sent to her by her parents—archeologists studying Mayan ruins. A strong dose of their powers might be just what she needed to get out of the mess she was in.

When Max Martinelli had owned the Chocolate Boutique, Chloe convinced him that displaying the tools and bowls would bring the store good luck and prosperity. Shortly after they were mounted on the wall, Chloe and Max created an award-winning bittersweet chocolate ganache made with wild raspberries. Max retired a few years later to sail around the Caribbean with his ex-partner, Sal. Every year on his birthday she sent him a box of the raspberry ganache. It was still her best seller.

The beauty parlor ladies and Sarah might believe that they had the answer to her problem. Chloe knew the solution would come from the chocolate.

She would honor her agreement with Sarah, but there would be no still-warm-from-the-oven chocolate chip cookies for any of her future dates. She pushed aside the thought of all the Henrys she would meet and concentrated on the one man who might become something of a problem in the next few weeks.

Chloe suspected it would take more than the power of a heaping tablespoon of her best cocoa to sidetrack a man like Ethan Behar.

Let him come. She would give him the best she had. She was more than ready to take on the challenge and save the tenants in her Aunt Bessie's building from whatever fate Ethan had planned for them. Maybe she'd even name a chocolate after him.

Chloe glanced at the display case. What kind of chocolate reminded her of Ethan Behar? It would most likely be a strong, bittersweet blend that hit your senses with the first bite.

Chapter Three

Ethan was a fool to continue pursuing this sale, but he had already invested large sums of money, and it wasn't in his nature to pull out of a deal. Too many supporters had willingly put up the funds needed to make this project succeed. What would they say if they knew that the deal was on hold because of a sassy little chocolatier with spiked pink hair?

All this was just a little bump in his path. He was becoming bored with easy acquisitions and wasn't about to back down from the challenge this one offered.

He might have underestimated Chloe Brandeau, though. Interesting, spunky, and definitely pleasing to look at, she was going to be the challenge he needed to get his juices flowing.

More than any of her obvious attributes, he saw something that he found lacking in most of the women he knew. The Chocolate Lady had nerve and determination. Very few people, men or women, had the nerve to meet him head-on, question him, or outright refuse to listen to what he had to put on the table.

Women were never an issue for men like him. They were plentiful, always hoping to be the next Mrs. Behar. Ethan had made that mistake once and would never do it again. He had been young, foolish, and what he had thought, at the time, in love.

His ex-wife had fallen in love with the man he had become and wanted nothing to do with his life before they met. The youngest son of a New York City transit worker, Ethan had learned his work ethic and drive from his family. Most people did not realize that his past was still as much a part of him as his success.

A moan from the backseat interrupted his thoughts. Next to him, Brad hummed along with the radio.

"How you doing back there, buddy?" Ethan looked over his shoulder at the hot dog lying across the backseat.

Henry mumbled something about feeling better. "Why don't you take me back to my corner so I can finish working?" He nudged the back of the driver's seat with his foot.

"Sorry about that. Ethan wants you to be seen by a

doctor before I drive you anyplace." Brad lowered the radio.

"Do you always do what he tells you?" Henry twisted on the seat.

"He's the boss." Brad chuckled, then asked, "From one working guy to another, what do you do when you're not a hot dog?"

"I do handyman stuff, and sometimes on weekends I dress as an ice cream sundae," Henry replied. "It's only temporary, until my home-repair business takes off."

Ethan nodded. He understood that everyone had to make a living. What he couldn't figure out was Henry's connection to Chloe. One minute she seemed annoyed by his presence and then a bit too concerned, but most of the time she'd tried to ignore the giant hot dog.

Ethan had been aware of her eyes on him most of the time: scrutinizing, assessing, and waiting for him to make the wrong move. Was that how she worked? Had she lured his men into her store and hit them with just the right dose of her chocolate charm to bring them down?

Ethan ran a hand through his hair. An image of the sexy little chocolate maker took over his thoughts. "Henry, how long have you known Chloe Brandeau?"

"I've seen her around, but we met officially last night."

"Last night?"

"It was a blind date." Henry lifted himself to a sitting position, squishing the top of his bun into the roof of the SUV. "She doesn't know, but I know all about her agreement with the matchmaker."

It was difficult to take this talking hot dog seriously, but even more amusing was the idea of the quirky lady with the sexy legs needing a matchmaker. "Chloe has a matchmaker?"

"Sarah's an accountant who does some matchmaking on the side. She refers to herself as a dating consultant. Sarah's not working in her official capacity for Chloe. It's more like a favor to a friend."

"So Chloe asked her friend, a dating consultant, to make a match for her?" The whole idea of Chloe's hiring a matchmaker intrigued Ethan. "This must be a pricey arrangement."

"She's not charging Chloe." Henry said. "The whole thing was Sarah's idea—to find Chloe a husband to help her out of her current financial mess."

Ethan refrained from smiling. His reports were always on target. This time was no exception. His representatives had informed him that Miss Brandeau was in over her head when she inherited that run-down old building.

"Are you set up with this dating consultant too?" Ethan asked.

"I can't afford Sarah's accounting *or* matchmaking fees." Henry hesitated a moment.

Ethan's bargaining skills had taught him that hesitation signaled that his opponent had more to say. "So how did you end up dating Chloe?" Ethan prompted him.

"Sarah does some pro bono accounting at the senior center where my mother volunteers."

"So your mother arranged the date?" Ethan ignored Brad's snicker.

"I was at the senior center doing some odd jobs and overheard Sarah and my mother discussing Chloe." Henry shrugged. "Chloe set a time limit on Sarah's offer. She only has until May, when Chloe goes to the Chocolate Ball. Sarah wanted to get things going, so I offered my services as Chloe's first date."

Ethan never liked to appear too eager, but this information might prove useful. At the moment he had to make Henry trust him, encourage him to talk. "She seemed very concerned for you. I think she likes you."

"You think so?" Henry tried to puff out his chest. As if he could look manly stuffed into that ridiculous costume.

Ethan was no fool. He had sensed that Chloe's overweening concern for Henry was really redirected contempt she felt for him. Winning a popularity contest was not Ethan's goal; buying her building was. "Tell me about this matchmaker's plan."

"Sarah is a romantic and believes that everyone's problems can be solved by meeting the right partner.

Chloe's only giving Sarah three chances to find her the right date by the time the Chocolate Ball rolls around."

Ethan strained for a better look at the hot dog philosopher. He couldn't disregard what he had to say. The man might have more insight than he knew. "Do you think Chloe agreed to this plan because she wants a date for the ball or because she wants to hook up with a man for financial security?"

"I don't know her that well, but I know she'd never date someone for his money. There's something about her, like her hair. It's kooky but attractive."

"I have to give her that one. She's definitely got her own ideas on how to do things." Ethan smiled. She had somehow managed to turn his day completely upside down.

"I think she agreed to this dating scheme just for the heck of it. We had fun, but I got the feeling she's not really looking for a serious relationship," Henry said.

"Only three chances?" Ethan appreciated the constraints that Chloe had on her agreement with Sarah. He imagined other women might allow Sarah to supply them with an endless list of eligible men, searching forever for something that didn't exist.

"You've heard the expression, boss." Brad added his two cents. "Third time's the charm."

"And if Sarah fails?" Ethan ignored his driver and looked at Henry out of the corner of his eye. "If none of her selections charm Miss Brandeau, then what?"

"I don't think Chloe is concerned."

Henry might look ridiculous, but he seemed like a sensible guy. He was just in a dead-end job and had picked the wrong girl.

"And Cinderella goes to the ball alone," Ethan stated matter-of-factly.

"I guess so, if none of her dates work out." Henry sighed. "I could take her if she'd like."

"Hey, boss. Maybe you could hook up with this matchmaker." Brad pulled up in front of the emergency room at County Hospital.

Ethan turned to his driver. "What makes you think I need her services?"

"You could sacrifice yourself for the good of the kingdom. It's been done for centuries. Date the lady of the manor for profit and gain."

"Since when did you become so ruthless about romance?"

"I watched an old movie last night, and it got me thinking how relationships haven't changed much." Brad hummed a tune Ethan didn't recognize.

"What a great movie." Henry started to hum along. Obviously he was an old-movie buff like Brad.

It wasn't that Ethan didn't appreciate Brad's passion for the movies; he just didn't have time for such trivial pursuits. "As you said, that stuff happens in the movies.

This is real life. Wheels turn, deals are made, and money flows."

"Money, money. Haven't you heard it can't buy love?" Brad's eyebrows lowered, and in the backseat Henry released a long, exasperated sigh.

"What's with you guys? I feel like I'm surrounded by a bunch of Dr. Phils. Don't you know you can't trust love, that it never has a good ending?"

Henry attempted to lean forward, showing interest in the conversation. "You're not married?"

"Divorced." Ethan said. "And it cost me a lot more than the price of the ring."

"Too bad." Henry's top-heavy bun bobbed in Brad's direction. "Even if your boss believed in love and all that stuff, trying to date Chloe is never going to work."

"Why not?" Ethan snapped around before Brad had time to respond. No one ever told Ethan Behar he wouldn't succeed—until today.

"Let's be honest." Henry suddenly spoke with authority. "Even if you decided to use Sarah's services, Chloe doesn't like you very much."

"You're missing the point." Brad shut off the engine. "Chloe could get to know Ethan on an entirely different level. You know what I mean. Boy and girl get together, they don't really like each other, but something big happens, and you know the rest."

"And then what?" Henry asked with an uneasy edge to his voice. "He goes in for the kill?"

"I've known this guy a long time." Brad placed a hand on Ethan's shoulder. "Under this tough façade is a really sensitive man in touch with his feelings."

Ethan removed Brad's hand. "Don't give me that metrosexual nonsense you've been reading about." He opened the car door. "Let's get this guy into the ER."

Ethan and Brad attracted a small crowd of hospital staff as they inched Henry out of the backseat. The poor guy seemed smitten with Chloe, wanted to protect her, but how much financial security did someone like Henry have to offer? After meeting the sassy chocolate maker face-to-face, Ethan could almost understand Henry's feelings. Sexy legs and chocolate could be a deadly combination. Luckily for Ethan, he had the willpower to avoid such decadent temptations.

Chapter Four

Two weeks into the month of April was too late for Mother Nature to be playing an April Fool's joke on the city of New York. Last night's unexpected snowstorm had not only blanketed the streets in a foot of snow, but also left Chloe's tenants without any heat.

Expecting an early spring, Chloe had taken the chance and decided not to spend the little money she had left in her savings account to tune up the old furnace. Realizing after the fact that she had made a bad decision was something she had been doing a lot of lately. How was she supposed to know the night of the storm would be the night the old burner stopped working?

Fortunately for her, Henry had decided that even

though they were not romantically compatible, they could still be friends. Her new friend happened to be surprisingly handy with a toolbox and eager to earn money from the odd jobs she needed done. A desperate call to him at midnight and a few twists and turns later, he had the furnace growling like Mrs. Katz's new real-live bulldog puppy. She made a mental note to remember to send him a box of his favorite chocolates along with his paycheck.

Leaving her tenants warm and snug in their beds, Chloe started out early for her shop. The sudden April storm might not bring May flowers, but it would bring customers into her shop for a cup of her frothy hot cocoa.

Chloe dressed in layers with her favorite well-worn jacket, a cotton-candy–colored faux fur, on top. A pair of sheepskin boots she had recently purchased at an end-of-the-season sale kept her warm as she trudged along the slippery sidewalks.

Light traffic crawled along the already slushy streets. Heat from the subway below had turned the pristine snow to a wet, caramel-colored slush.

Inside her shop the familiar smell of chocolate welcomed her. She replaced her wet boots with a pair of tall, crocheted slip-ons. She pulled them up over her skinny jeans just as the bell over the door announced the first customer of the day.

"If you're here for a cup of hot cocoa, I'm sorry,

you'll have to wait." She turned and found herself face-to-face with the last person she had expected to see out and about on a morning like this.

Ethan Behar stood in the doorway, stomping the snow off his boots.

"I'm not a big chocolate fan, but anything hot sounds good in this weather." He removed his jacket and tossed it over the back of a chair.

What was he doing here so early on a morning like this? She hadn't seen or heard from him since the morning Henry had bled all over her sidewalk. Was he here, as he had said he would be, to take care of their unfinished business? Did he suspect the sudden storm had compounded the issues with her money pit? Had he come to make a deal when he thought she was down?

Chloe looked directly at him and wanted to believe that even the master of acquisitions was not that despicable. She'd have to soften him up the only way she knew how.

"Don't worry Mr. Behar, even you'll find that my cocoa warms more than just your cold body."

"Please call me Ethan." A sly smile curled his lips.

"What brings you out on a morning like this, Ethan?"

"Snow puts a damper on construction. Not much going on this morning. I've come to see for myself how good you really are." He adjusted his jacket on the chair and took a seat. "I'm looking forward to sampling that magical brew I've heard so much about." His watched her as she moved toward the counter.

From her vantage point behind the display case, she had a good view of him. Dressed in a gray sweater and jeans, he looked more like he should be on the cover of a skiing magazine than of *Financial Times*. She found it difficult not to be attracted to this man. If she put aside his unrelenting desire to purchase her building and turn the block into unaffordable condos, she might find him likeable. He had an easygoing, I'm-comfortable-anywhere attitude. And his cologne or aftershave had the most intoxicating lemon scent she had ever experienced. She understood that liking anything about him was not a good idea.

While she gathered her supplies, Ethan walked around the shop. He joined her behind the counter and studied the wall displaying the old chocolate-making tools. "These are Mayan?"

Most people were interested in the artifacts. Why should Ethan be different?

"How do you know they're Mayan?" Chloe poured milk into the frother without turning away. A small drop dribbled onto the counter.

"I took an archeology course when I was in college."

"Oh, a minor detail your interviewer left out," she retorted.

"Most people aren't interested in my past. They're more concerned with what I'm up to at the moment. The readers want information that will tell them what's the newest up-and-coming neighborhood and who's buying what and where." Ethan reached for a napkin and wiped up the spilled milk. "A little background and family stuff is just so much fluff for them."

Hmm. That family stuff had gotten *her* interest. "What are you up to now, or do I have to wait for the next installment?"

"That all depends on where the deal between us goes. You might have a better idea of what's going to happen next than I do."

"There is no deal between us. My building is not for sale." Feeling much too close in the confines of the small space behind the counter, Chloe shifted from foot to foot. She looked up at him and added, "Unfortunately for you, no one has written an article giving you any insight into who or what *I* am."

"You might be surprised at what I know." He studied the sign mounted below the relics. "Donated by Emma and John Brandeau." He turned away from the plaque and said with an air of authority, "Emma and John are professors at UCLA. They have one daughter, Chloe." He looked down at her with a raised eyebrow, a challenge. "Am I right so far?"

"Good guess." She shrugged and ran her fingers over the raised letters on the wall plaque. A restless surge made her want his attention to turn away from her. She read the words out loud. "These artifacts are on loan to the Chocolate Boutique."

"I'm not guessing. I've got an excellent research department." He placed a finger under her chin, turning her face toward him. "Chloe Brandeau, thirty years old, the only child of Emma and John, resides at 130 Butler Street. She has an undergraduate degree in business and is a graduate of the Ecole du Chocolate." He smiled. "Should I continue?"

"It's not necessary. You've gathered the basic facts." Not many people knew she had a business degree. She had always felt comfortable and secure in her shop, but now she felt awkward and strange.

"Very basic." He nodded. "There are some things I prefer to learn on my own."

Chloe chose that moment to reach up for her special chocolate pot. Standing on tiptoe and overstretching sent her sweater up an inch or two above her abdomen.

Ethan stepped back and swiped a finger across his chin. "Now there's a bit of info that even my researchers would never know." His gaze traveled to the golden ring dangling from her belly button.

Chloe had never felt so exposed or so vulnerable. She took a breath, conscious of the slight rise and fall of her stomach and the movement of the gold ring. Her skin quivered from his gaze. She needed to escape.

She turned away and placed the pot on the counter. Her sudden movement caused her shoulder to unhinge a Mayan bowl. A resonant sound echoed in the shop as the bowl made its way down the wall.

Chloe reached for it. Ethan, now standing behind her, reached around her. He closed his hands over hers, securing the bowl between their fingers. She felt his breath on her neck. Even through the thick layers of his sweater and jeans, his closeness disturbed her more than if he had touched her bare skin. Her heart began to pound, and she clenched the bowl. He did the same, tightening his hold on her fingers.

Spheres of chimes continued to sound. The ringing, so ancient and powerful, kept Chloe riveted to her spot. She had never experienced anything like this when handling the artifacts.

After what seemed like forever, the chimes toned down to a still silence. Ethan recovered from the experience first. A change in the pressure of his hands made her relinquish her hold and step forward.

She walked away and dashed to the front of the counter, leaving the chocolate-filled display case as a barrier between them. While she finished preparing a cup of her special cocoa, Ethan hung the bowl back on the wall.

"That was close." Ethan rubbed the back of his neck. "That's the chance your parents take displaying these kinds of artifacts in public."

"My parents prefer to display their finds where everyone can enjoy them."

"Thank them for me the next time you speak to them." He gave her a smile that sent her pulse racing. "Their little treasures definitely offer an unusual but enjoyable experience."

"Whatever." She had hoped he wasn't going to make any reference to what had just happened. "The artifacts are here on loan instead of being catalogued away in some dusty university or museum basement."

"Does your chocolate pack that kind of punch too? If it does, I can understand how my agents got side-tracked."

"It didn't take much to distract your men from their main purpose." How dare he insinuate that she'd had a similar experience with the men he had sent to offer her a deal? She concentrated on adding just the right amount of cocoa powder to an oversized white mug. Ethan Behar was definitely the kind of man who did things in a big way. No small, delicate, porcelain cup for this man. She smiled at the image. She'd charm him with a healthy taste of her decadent beverage. "Have a seat, Mr. Behar."

"Ethan," he reminded her. He took the mug and straddled a chair at the window table.

Steam rose in soft curves above the cup.

"One marshmallow or two?" Chloe didn't wait for an answer. She plunked one fluffy white marshmallow into the cup. She had determined at their first meeting that Ethan was not the type to overindulge in sweets, although he could probably use a big dose. Why waste her handmade confection on someone she doubted would appreciate the time and effort that went into its making?

She watched him inhale, filling his nostrils, before he put his lips to the mug. Feeling as if she was intruding on a personal experience, she tried to look out the window. His image was reflected in the glass, however, and she was forced to watch him take his first sip. She knew he wouldn't be able to resist the velvety liquid. He held it in his mouth before swallowing. She watched his Adam's apple bob in his throat when he finally did.

For a moment she thought she had him. He was not the only one with tactics. Would he succumb to the power of her chocolate, humble himself, and admit that he had made a mistake? She might then be able to convince him, as she had his agents, that the purchase of her building was not going to happen.

"So, what do you think, Mr. Behar?"

"I'm not a chocolate fan, but the aroma, the taste, the feel in my mouth, it's overpowering. I'm impressed." He looked at her with respect, the way he would an adversary worth his effort.

Chloe's ego rarely surfaced, but she felt she had won a small victory. Everyone had a weak spot for her chocolate, and the all-powerful Ethan Behar was no exception.

Ethan's BlackBerry dinged. Clasping his hands around the still-warm mug, he pushed it to the center of the table. He looked relieved when the sound broke the silence.

"Aren't you going to finish your drink?" She glanced at his still-full cup of cocoa and watched as he checked his message. "Is something wrong?"

"No. Nothing is wrong. The cocoa is unbeliev-able." He looked around the shop and stopped when his eyes came to her. "Everything in here is unbeliev-able." He picked up his jacket. "I've got to go. How much do I owe you?" he asked.

"It's on the house." Chloe managed what she hoped was a gracious nod. She swallowed hard, hop-ing not to reveal her disappointment, and busied her-self with clearing the table.

She placed the mug, napkin, and long-handled spoon on a tray. The doorbell sounded, and she knew that when she looked up, Ethan would be gone.

Ethan paced to the corner and back in an attempt to walk off his excess energy before getting into his car. The message on his BlackBerry was not as im-portant as he had made it seem, but was just the inter-ruption he needed to get out of the shop while he still had his wits about him. He took several deep breaths, filling his lungs with the cold air. The scent of Chloe's intoxicating potion still lingered.

What would a little chocolatier with pink-frosted hair have in her arsenal that he couldn't handle? He should have been more aware. If he had, he might not have fallen for her wide-eyed innocence.

After experiencing firsthand a sample of her chocolate charms, he couldn't dispute the reports his agents had prepared. They were right on target, referring to what they called "the Chocolate Lady's magic." This deal needed to be closed quickly and to his benefit. He had too much invested already. The deal for the ironworks building, although a good deal, had been more costly than expected, but his attorney had assured him the other landlords on the block did not know the true value of their property. By starting with the building that appeared in need of the most repairs, he had thought he would have an easy acquisition. He would be doing its landlord a favor. The other offers would fall like dominos once Chloe sold. Ethan now knew, he had misjudged Chloe.

There was still the possibility that the dating consultant would come through with a suitable match for Chloe. As ridiculous as the whole matchmaking scheme seemed, there was always the chance that someone wealthy would appeal to the Chocolate Lady. Ethan tried to imagine what such a man would

be like. Aside from being able to offer financial sta-
bility, he would have to be strong, determined, and
able to resist her charms, or he would find himself
catering to her every wish. He smiled at the thought
of fulfilling her desires and wondered how many of
her dates would have the opportunity to discover her
secret belly-button ring.

A change in tactics was what he needed. Ethan
had stored the information Henry had given him. He
compiled a mental list of the eligible men he knew.
There were a few who would be willing to help him
out by dating Chloe. He quickly dismissed the idea.
None of them seemed to fit his requirements.

Too bad she disliked him. He shook his head and
thought of the unusual moment they had shared hold-
ing the Mayan bowl. No, even if she liked him, he'd
still be in trouble.

Now more than ever he needed to keep a rein on his
emotions, to take advantage of his competence and
confidence and concentrate on the profitable, necessary
objective. After all, he was not without a few charms of
his own.

Chapter Five

Chloe cleared the table and noticed a crisp five-dollar bill lying under the sugar shaker. She had had no intention of charging Ethan the usual three dollars for a cup of her hot cocoa. Ethan, it was obvious, had thought otherwise, leaving her a more than generous tip. Business was, after all, business, and should not be confused with anything else. This was as good a time as any to develop her new selling philosophy. She couldn't make money if she served free hot chocolate.

With the bill still in her hand, she walked to the window. She watched Ethan stride to the corner. Where was he going? His car was parked directly in front of her store. He had definitely acted a bit odd this morning.

She refrained from stepping too close to the window. With a shrug she dismissed his strange behavior. Maybe it was the weather. Unexpected climate changes had a strange effect on people, even the predictable ones like Ethan Behar.

She turned and headed to the back of her shop. There was work to be done. Chocolate bunny and Easter egg molds had to be to prepared for her assistant, Lucy.

Even more important, there were Heavenly Truffle cups to make. Her customer flow might be slow today, but Chloe couldn't disappoint her regulars who would brave the slushy streets for one of her midweek specialties.

Making the award-winning candies was her favorite part of the week. The melt-in-your-mouth delicacies had taken second place at last year's New York Chocolate Ball. This year's event was a little over six weeks away. Chloe had been so consumed with her current problems, she hadn't been able to start preparing her entry.

On the pristine counter she lined up her mixing bowls. Considering her current economic crunch and low customer flow, she decided to make half the usual amount of truffles.

Seated on a stool, Chloe had full view of the front

door. She lined up all the ingredients in front of her. She did a mental calculation of the cost of the end product and her profit margin. Ethan would be impressed with her thinking. It might do him good to realize that you can't always have the entire chocolate bar or everything on the block.

She measured just the right amounts of whipping cream and fresh butter. Saving the best ingredient for last, she handled the Valrhona chocolate with the care and dignity it deserved. The melted bars would blend perfectly with her secret ganache flavors. Placing just a dab on the edge of a spoon, she did a taste test.

"Oh, perfect," she sighed. If only her life were so easy to put together.

When the ganache was finished, she separated it into three bowls, leaving one untouched for her customers who preferred their chocolate straight. To the next bowl she added a touch of crushed black pepper. She mixed and blended until the spicy ingredient was evenly disturbed.

To the last bowl she added a few drops of champagne and cinnamon. Surrounded by a mix of sweet and spicy aromas, it was easy to forget how her day had started.

She put the bowls of the creamy blends aside so they could set. They might not look like much, but once the ganache balls were set in her delicate dark-chocolate cups, few people could resist. Many of her customers were chocolate experts, interested in its finer points. They knew the origin and percent of cocoa in her chocolate. Unlike Ethan, they allowed themselves the decadent pleasures of her treats and velvety smooth hot cocoa.

He had been the only person to ever resist her cocoa and would most likely disregard her wonderful truffles as nothing more than a piece of candy. Was it even a reference point for someone like Ethan to know that chocolate produced the same chemical in the brain as the one released when you're in love? Her mental list of facts about chocolate was endless. She wouldn't be surprised at all if a man like Mr. Behar was chemically imbalanced for love. She knew his type, always reaching for the forbidden fruit, setting goals for things beyond his reach, enticing her with his lucrative offers. An image of his strong, determined look reminded her that she *was* his latest challenge.

The next step, creating the Valrhona chocolate cups, required concentration. The correct fat, melted to the right temperature, had to be added to the chocolate at just the right moment to effect the heat resistance and melting point of the finished product. The velvet-smooth feel of the first bite, combined with the taste of the ganache filling, were the selling points of the cups.

Chloe poured the melted chocolate into a bowl and gently whisked along the sides as she prepared to add the shortening. The store was quiet, and outside the sidewalks were absolutely still. The sun attempted to break through. Icicles dripped from the overhangs like melted sugar.

An occasional siren interrupted the silence. Chloe concentrated on the gentle sound of the whisk against her metal bowl. Today she could feel the rhythm of its movement. Not quite as intimate as the Mayan bowls, but definitely rhythmic in its own right.

"Oh, my ganache." Chloe realized, too late, she had added milk fat instead of cocoa butter. She jumped off the stool, jolting the utensils across the table. "What was I thinking?" She stared at the bowl.

The differences in the fat would change the melting point of her chocolate. She had never made such an expensive mistake.

"There's only one explanation. Ethan Behar." She had been thinking about him and the Mayan bowls. "This is all his fault." She looked down at the bowl. Maybe that had been his plan all along, to come into her shop and upset her day.

There would be no chocolate truffle cups today, but maybe she could still salvage some part of this disaster. She placed the soft filling in the refrigerator. When the ganache hardened, she would coat the balls with nuts or a blend of curry powder. That would work. But what about the ruined Valrhona?

She looked around the small work space, and an idea came to her. She reached under the counter and found a pastry bag. She filled it with the not-so-perfect blend and dropped bits onto a cookie sheet. At this consistency, they'd turn out better as chocolate chips than truffle cups. It wouldn't be one of her best products, but she could bag and sell the chocolate chips. Wasting ingredients was never good for her profit margin.

Chloe passed the next couple of hours completing the mindless task. She filled the entire work area with trays of chocolate chips. Like snowflakes, each had its own personal shape and size. When they set, she would bag them in crinkly cellophane and seal them with her pink-and-brown monogrammed ribbons.

The store bell rang. Chloe had been so engrossed in her work, she had forgotten that Sarah had promised to stop by today with a new selection of potential matches.

The weather had kept most people away, except, of course, for Ethan and a few die-hard chocoholics. "Time to take a break." She pushed the stool away from the counter.

"Who you talking to?" Sarah walked to the back of the store and looked around.

"Just thinking out loud."

"You look like you could use some help." Sarah nodded at the trays of chips ready for bagging. "I've brought some candy experts with me."

Chloe hated to admit that she might be beyond

help. She smiled when she saw whom Sarah had brought with her. Alex and Maddie were two of her best friends.

"You have no idea how nice your offer sounds." Chloe went to the refrigerator and removed the almost-hardened truffle balls.

"What happened to the chocolate?" Maddie gave Chloe a pitiful look.

Maddie, a native of Brooklyn, had attended Ecole du Chocolate the same year as Chloe. She was responsible for convincing Chloe to try her fortune in New York instead of returning to California. They had planned to open a shop together eventually, but Maddie found a job as a dessert chef in a posh Manhattan restaurant around the same time Chloe got hired by Max.

"What a mess." Alex, Max's granddaughter, had grown up around chocolate and knew a disaster when she saw one. When Max retired, Alex and her husband, Mike, had been Chloe's partners for a while.

Mike, a firefighter with a knack for baking, had found an opportunity to get in on the cupcake craze. He and Alex had sold their share of the chocolate shop to Chloe and opened a successful cupcake bakery.

Even though Chloe had exhausted most of her savings when she bought out their shares, the deal had been worth every cent. She owned something she had only dreamed about.

Thinking about Mike's cupcakes gave Chloe an idea on how to save her chocolate. She started gathering supplies. Assuming her friends wanted to help her out of this mess, she passed around jars of sprinkles and spices.

"Why don't we work out front?" She explained her plan to cover her blunder with colorful, tasty toppings.

"It's not like you to make such a drastic mistake." Maddie gave Chloe a cross look while she set up an assembly line of ingredients. "Don't worry. We won't let you waste this expensive chocolate." She coaxed Alex and Sarah into helping too.

Chloe stepped back and sighed. When had everything gone so wrong? Once again she watched her profits and her dreams to expand her shop slowly melt away.

Her profits from the upcoming Easter season would likely disappear with the purchase of a new furnace. At this point she was hanging on to both her shop and the apartment building by only a slight margin. She shook a colored sugar shaker a little too vigorously, covering a ganache ball with a generous coating of pink sparkles.

"Hey, don't overdo it." Maddie reached for the shaker.

"Leave her alone. Poor girl has a lot on her mind." Sarah walked away from the group and set up her laptop on the opposite table. She opened to a screen covered with thumbnail photos of men. "Take a break, Chloe. Let them finish the job. Come see who I've got in mind for your next date."

Chloe reached for the blue sugar, trying her best to ignore what Sarah had to say about date #2. Maddie refused to give Chloe back the shaker and urged her toward the computer screen.

Sarah was persistent. "I've compiled a group of men with interests similar to yours."

Chloe popped a handful of chopped nuts into her mouth and asked, "How do you know they're interested in meeting me?"

"Matchmaking is a science. I've shared your profile and photo with the best matches."

Unlike Chloe, these men were paying customers and had put together elaborate profiles. Chloe had answered the basic questions, allowing Sarah to complete the rest. She realized now that she should have taken a more serious interest in the process. Just a little curious, she tilted her head for a better look.

Sarah scanned through close to two dozen shots of men who had expressed an interest in Chloe. Chloe hated to admit it, but she was intrigued that so many men were interested.

"Take a closer look." Sarah nudged Chloe forward. "I'm confident you'll find someone who appeals to you. Look at their eyes. Research has shown that women are attracted to men for their eyes first. All that other stuff comes after."

Chloe wiped her hands on a towel and squinted at the small photos. She could barely make out their faces.

Sarah, noticing her friend's problem, hit the Slide Show button, but Chloe's concentration was somewhere else. She glanced briefly at each image that flashed across the screen. In each face she found something that reminded her of Ethan Behar: dark hair, taunting eyes, a flashy, corporate smile.

Many of the men seemed to force a style, a smile, or image that came naturally to Ethan. She had the feeling he always walked around with that air of confidence and authority, rather than assuming it for his magazine photo shoot.

She felt a pitiful disappointment at the thought that she might never see him again.

Sarah continued with her slide show. Each time an image changed, a soft musical note sounded, and a faint chime, almost tangible, moved through Chloe. She placed a hand on the table to steady herself, accidentally hitting the computer Pause key.

"Oh, you like this one." Sarah pointed to the photo Chloe had accidentally flashed on the screen.

He was a nice-looking man with a smile that showed more teeth than necessary. "Sure. He's fine."

Eager to get through Sarah's matchmaking with as little pain as possible, Chloe didn't look any farther.

"Good choice." Sarah shut off the program. "You'll have a lot in common."

"Yeah, right. You said that about my last date."

"Henry's sweet." Sarah smiled. "And don't you just love him in that hot dog costume?" She looked as if she had more to say but didn't.

Chloe was relieved that Sarah didn't elaborate about her date. She doubted Mr. Teeth would turn out to be Mr. Right. She just wanted to get through this date and the next one with as little hassle as possible.

"How's that Behar thing going?" Sarah asked while she fiddled with her computer. When she finished searching, she turned the screen around for Chloe to see. "Voila." From corner to corner was the cover of the *Financial Times* with Ethan's picture.

"Not funny." Chloe turned to walk away.

"Maybe he'd be interested in signing up with me."

"Sarah, I'm sure the man has a slew of accountants on his staff."

"I'm not interested in doing his accounts. I want him as a client for my dating-consultant service. Imagine the business I could get if word got out that he's one of my clients." Sarah looked at Chloe with a pleading look. "Maybe next time you see him, you can give him my card."

Chloe rolled her eyes. "He was here this morning, but I doubt I'll ever see him again." She glanced at Alex and Maddie. They had really gotten into decorating her sorry-looking truffles. Taking her suggestions a step further, Maddie drizzled multicolored stripes over the chocolate. Impulsively Chloe stepped forward, wanting to join them rather than continue her conversation with Sarah.

Sarah grabbed her arm, preventing her from walking away. "What did Mr. Behar want?"

"I'm not sure why he was here." Chloe let Sarah lead her toward a back table.

"Let's talk." Sarah sat down and signaled for Chloe to do the same. "As your accountant I have to tell you it might be in your best interest to call your cousin, Allen, and tell him what's going on. He might be willing to help you out. After all, his mother owned the building."

"You want me to ask him for money?"

"Why not?" Sarah pulled up Chloe's spreadsheets on her computer.

"I can't do that." Chloe didn't look at the computer screen. She didn't need to be reminded of her falling balance. She pulled a napkin from the holder and absentmindedly folded it into tiny squares. "Allen didn't seem too pleased at the will reading."

"Maybe he didn't know you were inheriting a nightmare." Sarah gave her a cautious glance. "Why didn't your Aunt Bessie leave him the building?"

"I was living with her when she died. I know how fond she was of her tenants. Allen always seemed annoyed by her connection to them. She must have understood he would sell or tear down the building the first chance he got."

Sarah nodded sympathetically. "That would leave you and all the tenants out on the street."

"Aunt Bessie made me promise not to sell the building unless everyone living there had a place to go." Chloe released a long, slow sigh.

The building was small, only four floors with six apartments to a floor. That didn't sound like too many tenants to relocate, until she considered the astronomical rents that were being charged in the area. Never mind her tenants; *she* couldn't afford to move.

"I thought it would be nice to own some real estate, but I was foolish to think it would be easy."

"Look." Sarah placed her hand on Chloe's. "Considering Cousin Allen is a hotshot lawyer, has he tried to get the building from you?"

"No. I hardly have any contact with him. You know, he's the kind of relative who sends you a card once a year." Chloe had to agree that Sarah had a point. Allen had the means to question the will, but he never had. "I think I'm on his office mailing list, because my Christmas card comes from the firm."

"Maybe his grim reaction was on your behalf. You must have had some kind of relationship."

"We were never close. His mother, Aunt Bessie, was twenty years older than my mother, and Allen has a good ten years on me." Chloe smiled at the memory of her saucy aunt with the big heart, who, like Chloe, had a passion for chocolate. "I spent my summers in Brooklyn while my parents were off on digs." She used the folded napkin to brush imaginary dirt off the table. "When I graduated from the Ecole du Chocolate, I moved here, Max hired me, and you know the rest."

"So, calling Cousin Allen is not a good idea?"

"I don't think so," Chloe said with a long exhale. "He's probably forgotten I even exist."

"What about your parents?"

"Absolutely not." Chloe stood and walked away. Sarah had no idea she had just hit on a topic even more sensitive than Aunt Bessie's building.

Chloe's parents had come to accept that their only child had chosen her own path. What they couldn't understand was why she couldn't make chocolate in California instead of New York. The demographics were not the issue. Chloe wanted to prove she could make it on her own. She had been doing fine until the Butler Street building became her problem.

And now, not only was the building a problem, but the man who wanted to buy it was occupying her thoughts.

Chapter Six

"Hi, darling."

Date #2 leaned against the door frame of Chloe's apartment. She had tried her hardest to postpone their meeting. The first week she'd claimed she had orders to fill for the upcoming spring holidays, and the next week she'd insisted she had to start her project for the New York Chocolate Ball.

Sarah didn't believe any of her friend's excuses and wanted nothing to do with Chloe's procrastinating. Once all Chloe's chocolate bunnies were in a row, Sarah insisted she call the man she had chosen and arrange her next date. Well, here he was.

The man with the bright smile actually had a name, Phil Webb. They had spoken briefly and arranged to have dinner at a local restaurant. It had been Phil's idea to pick up Chloe at her apartment. He'd wanted to do it right, show he was a gentleman. Assuming that Sarah would never set her up with a psychopathic stalker, Chloe had agreed to the arrangement.

She ushered him in before any of her nosy tenants happened to pass by and make a comment.

Phil stepped in and did a quick survey of his surroundings, then looked at her over the rim of his dark sunglasses. The glasses were the kind that motorcycle cops glared out of just before they handed you a ticket. He removed the glasses, snapped them shut, and flashed a smile so bright that Chloe almost asked to borrow his shades.

She hoped her get-me-out-of-here expression was not obvious, and she didn't appreciate his nod of approval. He proceeded to make himself comfortable in one of Aunt Bessie's overstuffed chairs. Chloe hadn't had time to change much in the apartment. The old, worn furniture didn't bother her; it provided comfort and memories she wanted to hold on to a little longer.

"Can I get you something to drink?" Chloe asked. She would have preferred leaving for the restaurant, but Aunt Bessie's hospitality lingered in the room.

"Got a beer?"

"Sorry, I don't. Only water or diet soda."

"Water's fine, if that's all you got."

Glad for a reason to leave the room, Chloe went

into the kitchen. She leaned her forehead on the re-frigerator door. "Sarah, I am going to kill you," she whispered to the cold, stainless-steel appliance.

"Who you talking to?" Phil stood behind her.

She straightened her shoulders and took a deep breath before turning to face him. "Bottle or tap?" She forced a smile. None of this was his fault. She had no one to blame but herself. She could have been more interested in the selection process. She only re-quired an honest, hardworking man. If Phil really were a police officer, he would fit that requirement, and it would explain his too-many muscles. Well, there'd be plenty of time over dinner to discuss their personal lives.

"Tap is fine." Phil walked to the sink and filled himself a glass. "You got a nice kitchen. You only see rooms this big in these old buildings." He leaned against the counter and scanned the room. "You did a nice job in here. Not so many tchotchkes, like you got in the other room."

The *tchotchkes* he referred to were Aunt Bessie's knickknacks. Too busy in the chocolate shop and with limited funds, Chloe had decided to concentrate on one room at a time. The kitchen, her favorite room in the apartment, was where she spent most of her time. On the rare occasion that she had some free time, she sat in the kitchen sipping a cup of her latest concoction while she scanned news articles about the candy industry. It was the only room where things were all hers: dishes, pots and pans, and stacks of her favorite magazines.

"I guess we should get going." Phil poured the remaining water into an overgrown plant on the windowsill above the sink. He placed the empty glass on the counter, looked at his watch, and added, "We've got a seven o'clock reservation."

Chloe had suggested Luigi's, a local restaurant that served candies from the Chocolate Boutique to all its dinner customers. If for any reason things were not going well, the waiters and kitchen staff would be there to help her out of an uncomfortable situation.

Chloe gathered her shawl, purse, and keys from the table by the door. She turned the multiple locks and was about to open the door when she heard a loud commotion on the other side. With her hand still on the doorknob, she turned to Phil.

He had a puzzled look on his face, but he gently moved her aside. "Let me take a look before we go out there."

Chloe didn't object. Nothing out of the ordinary ever happened in this building. She tried to make out the voices. Phil opened the door, and she peered around his wide shoulders.

Something or someone had upset Mrs. Katz's new bulldog puppy. With the little wrinkled dog cradled in one arm, the woman stood as a barrier between the building entrance and the small lobby. The little dog yapped at a shadow in the entrance.

Mrs. Katz turned when the door to Chloe's apartment opened. "Oh, dear, I'm so glad it's you. This man tried to get in without buzzing first. He tried to follow me in. He said he's a business associate of yours." She pointed a scolding finger in the direction of the man. "When Bessie was alive, things like this never happened."

Mrs. Katz stepped aside, giving Chloe a view of the intruder. While her eyes adjusted to the dim light, she made a mental note to have Henry put in brighter lightbulbs.

Chloe was already on edge, anticipating her dinner with Phil. It didn't take much to throw her over. "Ethan? Ethan Behar? What are you doing here?" Her voice came out several notes higher than usual.

He gave her a sly smile, shrugged, and said, "I stopped by your shop earlier, and the salesgirl, Lucy, said you took the afternoon off. I had business in the neighborhood and thought I'd stop by to see if everything was okay."

"I always take off Friday afternoons." Too late to take back her words, she knew she didn't owe Ethan any explanation as to why she wasn't in her shop.

Phil and Sadie looked at Ethan in a combination of

recognition and awe. No doubt they were wondering what had brought the infamous Ethan Behar here to mingle with the common people.

Phil and Sadie weren't the only ones curious as to why Ethan Behar would suddenly show up on her doorstep. She hadn't seen or heard from him since the day of the snowstorm. Yet here he was, all alone on a Friday evening, expecting her to greet him like an old friend who dropped in to check on her whenever he was in the neighborhood.

Sadie obviously had no patience for the silence. "Are you really that scoundrel who bought the ironworks down the block and wants to throw us all out into the street?"

"Sadie." Chloe couldn't believe Sadie's tone and choice of words, but it was funny hearing the matron of Butler Street call Ethan Behar a scoundrel. Chloe bit her lower lip to suppress her giggle.

Ethan took no offense at the lady's comment. He gave her a mock salute, flashed a smile, and said, "At your service, madam. But I have no intention of throwing anyone out."

Ethan held the door open as Sadie slipped past him. Her eyes darted to Chloe with a look of concern, then back to Ethan with contempt. The puppy in her arms attempted a threatening growl. Ethan chuckled and held up his open palms as they passed.

He seemed to be in a playful mood. Were things

going well down the street at his newly acquired property? Chloe wanted to believe that that wasn't the reason he was standing in her lobby—because he was eager to move along with his plans. She almost hoped he had really come to see her. She glanced at Phil and had a strange sense of déjà vu. This was beginning to mimic the morning Henry had bled all over her sidewalk and Ethan had shown up.

Phil, although not for the same reasons as Sadie, seemed to be just as affected by Ethan's appearance. He stepped forward and extended his hand. "Phil Webb." He flashed his bright smile. "Nice to actually see you, Ethan."

"Have we met before?" Ethan accepted the extended hand.

"We've never met, but we have some commercial interests in common." Phil clasped both hands over Ethan's.

Business, business, business. *Was that all men ever talk about?* Chloe felt the need to intervene. "Phil and I were just going out to dinner. I wish you had called." After the words were out, she realized she really meant what she had said.

Ethan needed to come here, only not at this moment, to see for himself that there was more to this building than brick walls. His meeting Sadie hadn't been such a bad thing. The encounter was definitely a flesh-and-blood experience. Chloe wished she had the time to invite him into her apartment so he could see that the building was also her home. The twenty-four apartments in need of repair meant more to her than the monthly rent checks she collected.

"I'm sorry. I didn't mean to intrude on your dinner plans." He cleared his throat and looked at her. "You look very colorful tonight."

His grin flashed across his handsome face, and she knew his observation was meant as a compliment. She pulled her shawl up around her arms, covering her shoulders and the straps of her multistriped slip dress.

"Hey, guy. Why don't you join us for dinner?" Phil's loud voice boomed in the small lobby.

"No thanks. I'll stop for something on my way home," Ethan said.

"You gotta eat. Chloe doesn't mind." Phil tapped her with his elbow. "Do you?"

Chloe hesitated. She was torn between the thought of spending another evening in the company of a man Sarah, for some bizarre reason, had thought was her perfect match and having Ethan there as a buffer. What would happen when Ethan discovered that Phil was an arranged date? Would he find her pathetic?

"You guys wait here." Phil was outside before either of them could object. "I'll bring my car around." Over his shoulder he explained, "I had to park around the corner."

Chloe offered no resistance when Ethan placed his hand on her elbow and guided her out of the building.

"Is he always like this?"

"Who?" Chloe asked.

"Phil. Does he always act so impulsively?" Ethan gave her a curious look.

"Oh, Phil." She released a nervous laugh. "I guess." She shifted her weight and looked down the street, anxious for Phil to arrive.

"I'd like to make some kind of association with how he knows me. What's he do for a living?"

Oh, boy. What had she gotten herself into? She should have objected to Ethan's joining them.

What if she said, *I think he's a policeman*? If she had allowed more time to chat with Phil before the commotion in the hallway happened, she might have an answer to Ethan's question. She didn't even know what her date did for a living. How lame did that sound?

Would she have to confess Sarah's ridiculous plan, leaving her open and vulnerable? Would Ethan take it as an opportunity, seeing how desperate her financial situation was, and zoom in for the kill?

She owed him nothing, but honesty was almost always the best policy. She would just have to tell the truth before any of it came out in their dinner conversation. She turned and found that Ethan had stepped closer. His dark eyes reflected the bright streetlights, and she forgot for a moment that she was going to tell him that she had never met Phil before tonight.

They looked at each other in silence, then Ethan said, "I really should go. I don't belong here, intruding in your private life. That's not how I do business." He looked at her with his chairman-of-the-board expression. He was in charge and calling the shots.

Chloe forced a sweet smile. "Of course you have to join us for dinner. You and Phil seem to have a lot in common. Neither of you can put aside the opportunity to talk business. Maybe the two of you would be even better off with a boys' night out." The idea appealed to her. She would prefer sitting in her kitchen reading a magazine. At least an evening at home, alone, had no potential for any mishaps.

She looked up at his face to see his reaction but was distracted by the white van coming to a stop at the curb.

"Hop in, guys," Phil called from the open window.

Ethan chuckled as he walked toward the van. "A Mr. Swifter van. You gotta love his marketing style."

At the moment Chloe was not loving anything. She stared, speechless, at the large toilet bowl brush on top of the van.

"That's how he knows me." Ethan indicated with a nod that he recognized the familiar logo. "I contract with his company for most of my office cleaning." He didn't seem at all bothered by the sudden appearance of the van with the hideous cleaning utensil stuck on its roof.

Phil jumped from the van and ran around to open the door for Chloe. She had to admire the man for his old-fashioned values.

"Sorry about the vehicle, but my car is in the shop."

With caution, Chloe dipped her foot over the threshold and slowly inched her way into the van.

"We'll all have to sit up front." Phil gestured to the backseat.

The assortment of harsh cleaning agents there assaulted Chloe's delicate senses. No wonder the man wore so much cologne.

Over her shoulder she noticed Ethan's expression. He smiled, trying hard to stifle a laugh. How could he be amused by all this?

"I bet you never rode in one of these." Phil slammed the passenger door shut.

"I see these trucks all over the city. You definitely have a clever ad agency."

There wasn't much room on the crowded seat. Ethan's right arm rested on top of the open window. His other arm stretched behind Chloe and rested on the back of the seat. His fingers brushed gently against her bare shoulder.

Faced with the option of leaning back against Ethan's arm or shifting closer to Phil, the toilet bowl cleaner, she leaned away from Phil, welcoming the scent of Ethan's wonderful citrus aftershave.

Like a strawberry dipped in chocolate, she blended perfectly into the nook of his arm.

Reality hit her. The more she rejected what Ethan had to offer, the closer to him she found herself.

Chapter Seven

Chloe experienced a moment of panic as Phil pulled the van up to the valet in front of the restaurant.

"No reason to waste precious time hassling with parking." Phil tossed his keys to a kid barely old enough to drive.

"Hey, man, is this going to self-destruct or something?" The young valet smirked.

"Just keep it clean and out of trouble." Phil didn't seem the least bit bothered by the valet's comment or the chuckles from the crowd.

Chloe tried to shrink between the two men as they walked toward the front entrance.

The reservation at Luigi's was for two. Dinner business was booming as usual. Waiters floated through the double kitchen doors with hands full of plates of steaming pasta and yeasty garlic rolls.

Fortunately the maître d' recognized Ethan. He had no problem accommodating them with a larger table. "Please have a seat at the bar while we prepare your table."

Chloe released a sigh of relief, grateful for Ethan's notoriety. The change in the number of diners would not create a problem. She led the way to the bar. Ethan followed, but Phil stopped to talk to the maître d'.

"Nice shine on your floor. Who does your cleaning?" Phil asked.

Chloe looked at Ethan and rolled her eyes. "Sorry about Phil." She almost added, *I had no idea he was Mr. Swifter,* but she kept her comments to herself for fear of having to elaborate on the entire blind-date thing.

"Don't apologize. I've got you all to myself." Ethan pulled out a bar stool. His hand exerted the slightest pressure on her lower back.

A strange sensation radiated from the core of her body. For a moment she imagined that Ethan and not Phil was her date. She almost laughed out loud when she realized she was actually thinking about dating. And the most unlikely man turned out to be the one she was thinking about.

Ethan waited for her to be seated before he signaled for the bartender.

"Hey, Chloe." The young man behind the bar greeted the new arrivals. "What'll it be? Your usual, a chocolate martini?" He acknowledged Ethan with a nod. "What about you? Want to try one too?"

"I'm not a big chocolate fan." Ethan gestured with one hand, making sure that the bartender understood him above all the noise. "I'll have mine straight."

The bartender prepared their drinks in front of them. He slid a chocolate martini toward Chloe, then looked at Ethan and asked, "Sure you don't want to try one?" He leaned across the bar and whispered, "You know, dark chocolate releases the same chemicals as love."

"I'll pass on the chocolate this evening."

"Have it your way, buddy," the bartender said, then winked at Chloe.

Chloe blushed and looked down at her glass. She wanted to hurl her coaster at the bartender and would have if Phil's booming voice hadn't announced from across the room that their table was ready.

Ethan ushered her through the crowded bar to the main dining room. Phil waved to them from a table near the back. "Over here, you guys."

All Chloe wanted was to be seated with as little commotion as possible.

"Chloe, dear." Ida and a group of friends were finishing their desserts at the table next to where Phil waited. "Aren't you the busy one tonight?" She glanced at Ethan and over her shoulder at Phil.

Luckily a passing waiter slipped between Chloe and Ethan. She had no idea how she would have explained Ethan's presence if she had to introduce him.

"The food here is wonderful." Ida watched Ethan maneuver his way around the waiter. "You already know that or you wouldn't have come here with your friends. Don't let them leave without trying your white chocolate with Luigi's blueberry tart."

"I'll keep it in mind." Chloe glided toward the table where her two dates stood waiting for her.

"Which one's her date?" she overheard.

"Nice-looking men."

"Do you think she'd like my nephew, Simon?"

Ida's friends' comments throbbed in Chloe's mind. Why hadn't she chosen a restaurant in a different neighborhood?

Chloe took a seat and pulled her menu close to her face, hoping the busybodies at the next table would finish their dessert and leave.

No such luck. Peering over the top of the menu, Chloe saw Ida walking toward them. Ida glared at Ethan and turned her attention to Phil. "You must be Chloe's most recent match."

If the bartender's comment hadn't turned Chloe's cheeks candy-apple red, Ida's blunt, outspoken remark did. Ethan must think she surrounded herself with crazy old ladies and lunatics. Sinking deeper into her chair, she rested her head behind the menu.

"That's me, Phil Webb. The only man this little chocolate drop will ever need." Phil reached across the table, lowered Chloe's menu, and winked.

Chloe stopped thinking that all this was just a nightmare and would soon be over. She forced a smile and decided to go with the flow.

There was no avoiding an introduction to Ethan. "Ida, have you met Ethan Behar?" Chloe held her breath and waited for the worst.

Ida did not disappoint her. Ida's eyes opened wide, and she said, "Not formally, but don't you remember I was having my hair done the day he pulled up in front of your shop and . . ." She gave Ethan a most disconcerting look. "Knocked down poor Henry."

Chloe was about to speak in Ethan's defense. After all, it had been Henry's clumsy costume that was mostly to blame.

"One of the beauty-parlor ladies." Ethan flashed his most charming smile and extended his hand. "Nice to meet you."

Ida glared at Chloe, giving her a look that was meant to remind her she was consorting with the enemy. Then she turned away with the same menacing look and acknowledged Ethan's hand with just her bony fingertips.

First Sadie and now Ida, but Ethan easily handled

the old girls with his calm, masterful attitude. He took his seat and signaled for waiter.

Phil engaged Ida in a conversation. "I know that beauty shop—222 Union Street. I do their heavy cleaning twice a month. If those girls don't sweep after every cut, those hairs are a real problem."

"I imagine so." Ida listened politely to what Mr. Swifter had to say. Out of the corner of her eye she watched Ethan and Chloe study a shared menu.

The waiter arrived. Not until he stood poised with his pen over his order pad did Ida appear to get the hint that it was time she said good-bye. Even then, she was not leaving without adding one more embarrassing remark. "I'm glad to see you're getting away from that store, Chloe. As much as we love your chocolates, there's more to life than business. Remember, dear, my friends and I know lots of eligible young men you might be interested in meeting."

Chloe reached for her water glass, took a sip, held the glass to her lips, and stared at the ice chips floating at the top. *Oh, my God. I'm pathetic, I'm desperate, and everyone knows it. Worst of all, Ethan knows it.* She didn't hear the waiter ask for her order. When she looked up, everyone was watching her.

"You feeling okay?" Phil asked. "You need to eat. Try one of these."

She opened her mouth to refuse, and Phil slipped in a bread stick. The assault of grease and garlic kept her mouth occupied while the men ordered—Ethan, the wine, and Phil, a family-style dinner.

Phil's choice of entrees—butter-and-olive-oil–soaked ravioli, parmesan fritters, and eggplant rollatini overflowing with creamy ricotta cheese—satisfied Chloe's need for fattening comfort food.

Except for a few moments while Chloe remained poised and breathless on the edge of her seat, thinking another one of the neighborhood yentas was about to approach the table, dinner turned out to be a surprisingly pleasant experience. The familiar faces that flashed by and smiled were nothing more than customers who recognized her.

Putting aside her paranoid moments, she might suggest to Sarah that dating two men at the same time was the way to go. Chloe liked not having to be the center of attention, although occasionally she would glance up and find Ethan looking in her direction. His expression appeared hazy with an unreadable emotion. If he had caught on to the whole blind date thing, he wasn't letting on.

Phil seemed happy enough to have an audience willing to listen to his most recent cleaning adventure. "You can't imagine how thrilled I was when I discovered a simple solution for removing sticky substances on office desks." Phil's fork rested in midair while he explained. "Dab a little vegetable oil or peanut butter on them, then let it sit before washing it off with soap and water." He gave a mock salute with his fork and added, "Cheap, efficient, and it makes me look like a cleaning genius."

Ethan shrugged politely and took a sip of his wine.

Chloe didn't expect Ethan to understand Phil's enthusiasm for his products, but she hated to admit that she did. Comparing cleaning agents to chocolate might seem like comparing jelly beans to fine Valrhona cocoa, but she understood Phil's sense of accomplishment. She shuddered at the thought that they actually had something in common.

When every last morsel of food was gone, Phil leaned back, crossed his arms over his chest, and said, "Chloe, can I ask you something?"

Chloe stiffened, unsure where this conversation would lead. "Ask me something?" *Oh, no*, she thought, *he's going to ask me how I know Ethan. Will Ethan then ask how Phil and I met?* Everything had been going so well.

"What's with Ethan and your oldlady friends?" Phil wagged a beefy finger.

Chloe released an exasperated sigh and turned slowly toward Ethan. She didn't want the evening to end in an uncomfortable situation. Ethan had turned out to be a pleasant dinner partner and hadn't once mentioned her apartment building.

"I'm not sure why Ida has any ill feelings toward

Ethan. The incident with Henry was an accident. Ida didn't see how it happened."

"Who's Henry?" Phil asked.

"Henry the Hot Dog. He's a friend." *And you're Mr. Swifter.* "No, he's not really a hot dog." *And you're not a toilet bowl brush.* The oddities of her blind dates were too similar. Ethan was the only normal part of the entire equation. "Henry just dresses like a hot dog." The scene was vivid in Chloe's mind, but she wasn't getting the story out clearly. She just wanted to change the subject. Listening to Phil explain the components of his cleaning concoctions was at least a neutral topic.

Ethan offered a more elaborate explanation. "Henry's costume was a little top-heavy, and he lost his balance. Poor guy fell over and split his head. He ended up with six staples in the back of his skull."

Ethan's version of the unfortunate event appeared to have left Phil even more confused. "You know a guy who dresses like a hot dog?"

"Yeah, we do." Chloe thought about it and turned to Ethan. "The whole thing must seem ridiculous to someone who wasn't there."

He responded with a nod and a deep chuckle that made her laugh out loud.

"Okay, I guess I had to be there." Phil reached for the dessert menu. "Tiramisu, anyone?"

Chloe had a better idea. "How about dessert at my shop?"

"Hot dog! I get to sample some of your sweet treats." Phil waggled his eyebrows. He signaled for the waiter to bring the check.

Chloe watched as Ethan reached into his pocket for his wallet. "How much do I owe you?" he asked Phil, ignoring her suggestion.

"Are you kidding? I invited you. It's on me." Phil tossed a credit card onto the table. "Are you up for dessert?"

"No. I'm going to pass." Ethan avoided looking at Chloe.

"Now, there's a man with willpower," Phil said.

Chloe knew all about Ethan's willpower. He was the only one she had ever met who could push aside her hot cocoa after only a sip. Wait. How had she missed it? That should have been a clue. He didn't dislike her chocolate; he had to struggle not to give in to its power. She pressed her lips together to keep from smiling.

The thought of being alone with Phil was not very appealing, but the possibility of getting Ethan into her shop again, to take care of unfinished business, was definitely attractive. She knew exactly how to convince him to come along.

"I think you've read Ethan all wrong. Actually he has no control at all when it comes to my chocolate." Chloe stood and held on to the back of her chair.

Ethan stepped over to Chloe. A wisp of hair dipped

across her forehead. The backs of his fingers brushed against her skin, putting the lost strand into place.

"You're mistaken, Chloe. I can handle anything you dish out." He had gotten the meaning. In a soft voice edged with a warning, he accepted her invitation. "I'm looking forward to sampling your chocolate again."

Chloe's knees went weak. She hadn't expected him to take her challenge so seriously. Then again, Ethan Behar never lost, and he didn't know how to be anything but serious.

He leaned closer and whispered in her ear. "Are *you* sure you're up to this?"

The closeness of his lips sent a tremor through her. What had she gotten herself into?

Chapter Eight

"Oh, my ganache." Chloe stood frozen in the doorway of her shop.

Nothing appeared unusual as Phil parked his van in front of the Chocolate Boutique. The street was deserted at this late hour except for a few stragglers. The shop's window twinkled with pink lights the same color as Chloe's frosted hair.

Chloe had to jiggle her key in the lock several times before it opened. She realized something was not right, but when she turned on the light, she knew exactly what was wrong.

Not only had someone messed up her perfect rows of candy in the display case, but an entire row of chocolate bunnies was missing from the over-head shelves.

"Chloe, is something wrong?" Ethan came up behind her, resting his hands on her shoulders.

Phil asked a similar question. Their voices were no more than a mumble passing through Chloe's mind. She couldn't respond. The shelves without the bunnies looked so sad and empty. The sadness was so acute, it hurt her physically to look at the vacant rows. She had fallen through Alice's rabbit hole and couldn't find her way out.

When she found her voice, short, fragmented sentences were all she could manage. "The bunnies—all done. Lucy helped me decorate them. Box them. Put them on the shelves." Chloe moved toward the bare wall.

Phil inched his way around her. He looked confused. "What bunnies?"

"I think chocolate Easter bunnies were supposed to be on these empty shelves." Ethan stood next to Chloe. He placed a hand on her elbow, offering her support. "Am I right?"

"Maybe this Lucy chick put them someplace else," Phil said.

Chloe managed to shake her head in disagreement while she stared at the empty surfaces.

"We should call the police." Phil snickered. "Tell them your bunnies hopped away."

"That's not funny," Chloe retorted. "These weren't just any Easter bunnies. They were made from Valrhona chocolate."

"Val . . . what?" Phil looked from Chloe to Ethan.

"Master French chocolate makers," Ethan said over his shoulder as he walked to the back of her shop. He opened the door to the work area and surveyed the space. "There's the entry point." He pointed to the broken lock on the back door, then bent down and retrieved a pastel foil wrapper. "This yours?"

Chloe looked at the wrapper and noticed another, then another, lying on the ground just beyond the door. Pink, yellow, and blue wrappers made a path down the alley. "My petite chocolate eggs too."

She felt a cold shiver down her spine. The sensation had nothing to do with the cool evening breeze from the open door. Some thief had not only stolen her precious bunnies but had also violated her sanctuary.

"Looks like the culprit left a trail." Ethan pulled out his cell phone. "Phil's right. We should call the police."

"No, not yet. I can't let this get out. There's only two weeks until Easter. If my customers find out, they'll demand their deposits back."

"So give them back their money." Phil looked over Ethan's shoulder. "It's not good business to deceive your customers."

"I can't." Chloe looked in Ethan's direction. She hesitated before explaining.

"You spent the money?" Ethan asked.

"I had to pay Henry to fix the furnace in my building." Chloe clasped her hands over her forehead and walked back to the front of her shop. "Who would do such a thing? Why would anyone steal my bunnies?"

"It could just be kids or a petty thief." Ethan still held his cell phone. "The bunnies were probably the most visible items here and the easiest to take. The culprit is most likely long gone."

"So why call the police?" Chloe asked.

"They might be able to recover the stolen merchandise," Ethan suggested. "Or it might not be an isolated incident, and by notifying the authorities, you would be helping the other merchants in the neighborhood. The decision is yours."

"You're right. We should call the police. But I wouldn't sell the bunnies even if they were found."

"Why not?" Phil asked.

"They might have been contaminated or tampered with."

While Ethan called the police on his cell phone, Chloe paced around the store, thinking out loud. "I need to find a way to get more chocolate. I could work day and night, and the bunnies could be ready in time for Easter."

"Sounds like a plan. Why don't you give this Valrhona guy a call and see what he can do for you?" Phil suggested.

Chloe spun around. "It's not that easy. You don't just call France and tell them you need some more couverture bars. In case you haven't heard, Easter is a big chocolate-eating season."

"Okay. It was only a suggestion." Phil pulled out a chair and sat down. "Sit down and relax." He pointed to the other chair.

Chloe couldn't sits; she had too much on her mind, and she thought best on her feet. She managed a weak smile for Phil's benefit. Poor guy, he certainly hadn't bargained for this when he hired Sarah as his dating consultant.

Ethan joined them. "There's a squad car in the neighborhood. They'll stop by and make a report." He flipped his phone off. "Phil might have an idea. You might be able to get some more Valhrona."

Chloe looked at both of them. If the chocolate was even available, the cost of reordering this close to the holiday would be far above her cost margin. But she wasn't about to share that bit of information with Ethan.

She didn't mean to raise her voice, but the words came out with an edge of annoyance. "The shipments go through distributors. I doubt they have any left. I'd be willing to bet . . ." She drummed her fingers on the counter and tried to think of something of value.

"How about your apartment building?" Ethan turned toward her with a wide grin on his face. "What is getting your hands on some chocolate worth?"

Chloe's irritation deepened. She felt the color return to her face, and her mind was working again. There was no question as to how Ethan had earned his reputation. He understood that this was about more than the missing bunnies. Her career as a chocolate maker was at stake. What else about her inner thoughts did he sense that she didn't want him to know?

She had just given him ammunition to bargain with. He was good. He never lost focus on the big issue. When he brought up her apartment building, her heart had bounced into her throat. And to think, for a moment this evening she had been dumb enough to imagine he was her date.

Chloe slipped behind the counter and reached for a tray of chocolate. This was her arsenal. "I was thinking more like a box of my most expensive candy. Care to try one?"

"Feeling better?" Ethan asked. "You've got your old spark back. I thought you might faint when you first came in."

"Looked like that to me too." Phil joined them. He reached for a candy. "If you're not gonna try one, I will."

Chloe tapped Phil's hand lightly. She put an

assortment of chocolates on a plate and placed them on the closest table. Phil followed the candy.

The front window suddenly became illuminated with the flashing lights of an NYPD squad car. The door opened, and two burly police officers entered.

"Someone call in a robbery?" the older of the two asked.

"I did." Ethan stepped forward.

"You own the place?"

"The lady is the owner." He nodded in Chloe's direction.

"What's missing?" The officer gave her a curious glance, starting with the tips of her hair. "You don't leave money in your register, do you?"

"No, they didn't steal any money. My chocolate bunnies are gone."

Ethan remained at the counter while Chloe explained the value of the missing candy.

"That expensive? Really?"

The younger officer pulled a flashlight from his belt and followed her to the back, where she showed him the candy-wrapper trail.

"Can you think of anyone who might want to hurt your business?" the policeman asked as they rejoined the group.

"No." With an odd twinge of uncertainty she glanced at Ethan. He was much too suave to resort to such a low tactic. She quickly dismissed the thought.

"You'll hear from someone in the morning." The officer handed her a copy of his two-line report. He tried to remain professional, but there was no denying that this was a story he would share back at the station.

They didn't seem to think the trail would lead them anywhere. Their entire investigation lasted only a few minutes. They had briefly questioned Ethan and Phil, taken a few notes, and given her a case number.

"Nothing else for us to do here." Phil took the remaining candies from the table and placed them in his pocket. "I guess I'll take Chloe home." He glanced at Ethan. "Need a ride?"

Chloe wasn't ready to leave, especially not with Phil. She had to tidy up the mess the thieves had left behind and secure her back door.

"I'm not ready to go home yet. Thanks for dinner." Chloe knew from her past experience with Henry to avoid encouraging Phil to stop by and say hello.

"How you gonna get home?"

"I'll walk. It's not far."

"Hey, I can't let you do that. I'd like to stick around, but I've got an early cleaning appointment."

"Don't worry. I'll see that Chloe gets home safely." Ethan said.

Chloe almost threw her arms around Ethan. He had saved her from having to get back into Phil's truck.

"Good night then." Phil winked at Chloe. "We'll be in touch."

Chloe felt strange being alone with Ethan once Phil was gone. She walked behind the counter and pretended to rearrange a row of dark chocolates. Her heart pounded foolishly. Annoyed with herself for allowing him to have this effect on her, she remembered he was only interested in what she represented to his growing empire.

Ethan leaned casually on his elbows and studied the display beneath the glass.

"See something you like?" Chloe asked. Silently she berated herself for letting the missing bunnies affect her so much, especially in front of Ethan.

"Give it your best shot. I wouldn't know which one to pick."

"I'd suggest you try one of these." She removed a special truffle in a dark chocolate Valrhona cup, her best chocolate.

Ethan toyed with the gold foil paper. "So, do you have a plan?"

"I do." Chloe straightened her shoulders and defied his dark eyes.

He leaned farther over the counter and asked, "Care to let me in on it?"

Grateful for the protective barrier between them, she said, "I can tell you for sure that it has nothing to do with offering my apartment building as collateral."

"Can't fault a man for trying." Ethan sounded so sincere. Chloe almost believed him, except now she knew better. "What's your plan?"

"Try my chocolate, and I might share my thoughts with you."

"Said the spider to the fly." Ethan's lips turned up in a playful smile. He took the tiniest bite and waited for her to continue.

"I have an old school friend, Maddie. She's a pastry chef, and she works with Valrhona chocolate."

He took another bite and asked, "You think she might have some extra chocolate lying around?"

Chloe responded with a nonchalant shrug. He had eaten half of the chocolate cup.

Ethan rubbed his chin and looked to be in thought. "A pastry chef? I might know of a few pastry chefs. Maybe we can make this a group effort."

With a sense of suspicion, Chloe fought the feeling of happiness that tried to surface. There might be a solution to her problem. Should she take the chance and let Ethan help her? She could wait for Maddie to check around, but what if Maddie's connections were limited? If she waited too long . . .

With trepidation she looked up at Ethan and asked, "What do you expect in return?"

"Only what you're offering." Ethan popped the remaining chocolate cup into his mouth. "A box of your best candies."

Chapter Nine

The weekend passed without any additional mishaps in Chloe's already topsy-turvy life. Maddie had called and apologized for not being able to help her friend out of her predicament, leaving Chloe still at a loss as to how she was going to fill her Easter bunny order.

"There's someone out front asking for you." Lucy, Chloe's assistant, peeked around the corner of the door leading to the work area. "Nice-looking guy with a package," she added, before she disappeared.

Chloe wiped her hands on a towel. Bunny molds filled with milk chocolate lined her work counter. They were no substitute for the stolen gourmet chocolate bunnies, but Chloe intended to give them, along with a refund, gratis to the customers she had disappointed. Her falling bank balance was so close to nonexistent, what harm would another withdrawal do?

She walked to the front of the store and found Lucy and the man with the package in a serious conversation about the Mayan bowls.

He turned to face her, and Chloe almost fell into the Easter egg display. From his eyes to his chin he was the image of Ethan. His features, however, were where the resemblance started and ended. Several inches shorter than Ethan, he did not require Chloe dangling to strain her neck to look at him. Unlike his impeccably dressed look-alike, he wore baggy striped chef's pants and a chef's jacket.

"Hi, I'm Ed Behar, Ethan's brother." He stared at her hair and said, "You must be Chloe." His eyes crinkled in a friendly smile. "Ethan sent out an SOS for some Valrhona." Ed held out a box. "I've got a few more of these in my car."

"You got the chocolate." Chloe reached for the package, unable to contain her excitement. She stopped in midair, her arms falling to her sides like solid chocolate. "How much?" she asked, and she held her breath, anticipating his answer.

"On the house."

"No way." Chloe glanced at Lucy, who shrugged.

"Why don't you take a look inside before you make any hasty decisions?"

"It's not Valrhona?" Chloe looked at the plain white boxes. There was no writing suggesting where the chocolate had come from.

"Oh, it's definitely Vahrhona. Go ahead, open it." He forced the box into her hands. "When Ethan came by José's on Friday evening, there happened to be a small contingent of chocolate chefs there." He must have gathered by her puzzled expression that she was confused. "You've heard of José's?"

"The after-hours tapas bar," she stated matter-of-factly. She vaguely recalled being there once or twice. What dumbfounded her was Ethan's being there. He did not seem like the type to hang out with off-duty chefs.

"That's the place. You've been there?" Ed asked.

"Yes, but I'm surprised that Ethan even knows José exists. He was here Friday evening. He did say he knew some pastry chefs. I assumed they worked at his favorite restaurants." She looked at Ed and smiled. It seemed so out of character for Ethan to have a brother who worked with chocolate.

"If you're surprised, you can't imagine how I felt when I saw Big E show up on his own in a place like that." Ed ran his fingers through his hair. "I figured it had to be something pretty important. You know, maybe something had happened to one of our brothers? Sounds like you know my brother pretty well."

"Oh, no. I don't know much about Ethan."

"He's always been a secretive kind of guy. Give him time. He'll open up."

Obviously Ethan hadn't explained their relationship when he went off to solicit chocolate for her.

Chloe was having a hard enough time digesting Ed's resemblance to Ethan. The idea of there being more Behar boys with their charming smiles was overwhelming. The *Financial Times* article had mentioned siblings, but she didn't recall how many. "How many of you are there?"

"Just four. Me, Big E, and two older brothers." He shrugged. "I guess you'd say Big E is the most successful. Not that the older guys are slackers or anything like that. They're both teachers. That's okay. It's honest work."

Chloe felt her mouth drop open. " 'Big E?' Is that how your family refers to Ethan?"

"Yeah, it's just something that stuck when we were kids. You know—Big Ethan, Little Ed. He was always a wheeler-dealer, even as a kid."

"I'm sure he was." Chloe imagined Ethan as a child negotiating with the neighborhood kids. She doubted that any of his affluent business associates were privileged to this information. Interesting as it all sounded, Chloe stored it away.

"Did they ever find the thieves?" Ed asked.

"Actually, it turned out that they weren't too hard to find." With the incident behind her, Chloe could see the humor in the situation. "They left a trail of candy wrappers, and the police found them a few blocks away."

"What kind of time do you get for stealing chocolate?" Ed laughed.

"They got off with community service. I didn't press charges—they were just kids."

"Your good deed deserves a box of Valhrona."

"I can't thank you enough for what you've done." She shook the box, jarring the contents. It was not as heavy as she'd hoped.

"No big deal. When Ethan told us about the robbery, the gang at José's really felt for you. Hey, we've all been there. You know how hectic it can get. You can make a mistake or fall short on an order."

"News travels quickly at José's. Lots of pastry and chocolate chefs hang out there. When they got wind of your story, they offered to dig into their stashes and help you out. There's no real way to say what the bits and pieces in the box are worth, but I'll bet they'll come together and make a bunny or two."

"There has to be something I can do to repay you."

"I'm glad to help out." Ed looked around the shop. "Maybe there is something you can do. The family is having a little birthday party for my mother this evening."

"No problem. Lucy will help you make up a box of our best." Chloe was only too happy to send a box of chocolates to Mrs. Behar. "Make sure you add some raspberry truffles," she instructed Lucy. Then she picked up her newfound treasure and started to walk away.

"That's not exactly what I had in mind." Ed followed her.

"You don't want candy?" Chloe should have suspected that if Ethan was involved, there had to be more.

"I do. But I'd like you to bring them to the house tonight."

"You want me to deliver the candy?" It sounded like a fair trade-off for rescuing her.

"Not like a delivery, more like a guest at the party. You see Big E–Ethan—doesn't share his personal life with us." He looked her over. "You're adorable and a real sweetheart for letting those kids off so easy. My mother would be thrilled to meet you." He hesitated. "A friend of Ethan's who's so down to earth, and all the trouble he went to for you. I don't remember his ever taking such an interest before. He doesn't even like chocolate."

"Oh, no, no. You have the wrong impression. Your brother and I aren't exactly what I would call friends." Ethan had simply orchestrated the Valrhona search. Poor Ed had no idea that his brother had negotiated the terms.

"He told me you two had dinner, came back here,

and the Easter bunnies were gone. If Big E's not working, he doesn't hang out with just anyone. My brother
has one, maybe two free hours a week, and he spent
them with you." Ed shrugged. "Sounds like you're
pretty special."

"That's just it. We weren't 'hanging out.' Ethan
and I are involved as . . ." How could she explain to
this sweet man who'd brought her Valrhona chocolate that she wasn't sure how to feel about his
brother? She didn't *want* to believe that this whole
chocolate rescue was only an attempt to soften her up
before Ethan hit her with another bid on her building,
but . . .

"Oh, I get it." Ed winked. "Even better. My mother
will be thrilled that he's involved with someone like
you."

Chloe was getting nowhere. Trying another approach, she said, "I've got a lot of work to do, Ed. I
really don't have time to attend a party."

Ed simply grinned. It was obvious he thought he
had found the best present anyone could give his
mother, and he was not taking no for an answer.

He reached into his pocket and pulled out an old
green-market receipt. He scribbled an address on the
back. "See you at seven."

Before Chloe could argue, he left.

Chloe stared at the crumpled paper in her hand.

Two steps out of the rabbit hole, and she had fallen back in even deeper. Going to the Behar house was not even an option.

"Where does the family live?" Lucy grabbed the paper from Chloe's hand. "I'll bet it's some fancy address."

Over Lucy's shoulder, Chloe glanced at the street. The Behars lived at a modest Cobble Hill address. The street was not far from her shop.

"I have an idea." Chloe walked behind the counter and opened her largest glossy white candy box. She lined it with pink and brown tissue paper and started filling it in an orderly arrangement. "Lucy, you'll make the delivery and offer my apologies."

"Oh, no. That is not in my contract."

"What contract? You work part-time. You've made deliveries before."

"You are as thick as frozen fudge." Lucy took the box from her and rearranged the rows of candy. "This is more in Sarah's line of work."

"You're right. I'll figure out what the Valrhona is worth and send a monetary compensation."

Lucy put down the box and turned to Chloe. "You have got it bad. Mention Ethan Behar, and you're like gooey taffy. You can't even think straight."

"This has nothing to do with Big—I mean, Ethan." Chloe took the box from Lucy. This time she picked out thick, dark chocolates with exotic spices. Ethan had actually eaten a piece of her candy last night, she remembered.

"It has everything to do with him. His brother thinks the two of you are dating and likes the idea. He's taking the initiative to move things along. So, move over, Sarah. Your matchmaker has some competition." Lucy elbowed Chloe with a playful nudge. "You're going to meet Mama."

"I'm doing no such thing." Chloe had no time to disagree. Lucy topped off the box, shoved it into Chloe's hands, and sent her out the door to prepare for her evening.

Chloe stayed on the bus, riding past the stop that would take her closest to the Behar home. The extra blocks gave her time to think of an escape plan should things not go well.

Still, before she knew it, she was standing on the first step of the stoop that led to the front door of the Behars' turn-of-the-century brownstone. *So this is where Ethan grew up?* The *Financial Times* article had mentioned that his parents still lived in the original family home. Much like her street, this neighborhood had once been populated by mostly blue-collar workers but was now sought after by young professionals.

Inching her way up the stairs, she thought of ringing the bell, leaving the box of chocolate, and making a mad dash for the corner. At the top of the stairs she stalled, her finger on the bell. She listened to the laughter drifting through the heavy wood door. With the lightest pressure on the bell, she pushed the button, hoping no one would hear.

The door opened. A little girl with a sequin-studded headband peeked out. "The pizza man's here," she announced. "But it's not a man. It's a lady with a big box."

Behind her a man—another Behar brother, Chloe assumed—ushered the girl away. "Go help Grandma. This isn't a pizza lady." His lips turned up in the same sly smile she associated with Ethan. "You must be Chloe." He extended his hand. "Hi, I'm Ernest."

"Yes, I'm Chloe, and I'm delivering these chocolates for your mother." She extended her arms with the box and prepared to turn and run, but a real pizza delivery boy came up behind her.

"Oh, no, you can't just hand me the box and leave. Ed said he invited you to the party." Ernest steered her past the door into a small foyer while he dealt with the pizza delivery.

The girl with the sequined headband now had a sidekick with the same dark-chocolate-chip-cookie eyes. The second girl wore an out-of-season Halloween T-shirt over a cotton-candy-pink princess tutu.

"I like your outfit." Chloe admired the child's independent style.

"You're pretty. What's in the box?"

"Chocolate."

"Chocolate pizza?" She looked up at Chloe with her big dark eyes.

"No, sorry." Chloe was glad she had added some simple chocolates to the box, even though it had never crossed her mind that there might be kids at the party. Did either of them belong to Ethan? It was possible. She had read that he was divorced. Keeping his children out of the limelight would be a smart idea.

"Daddy, we're going back upstairs," the girls announced to the man paying the pizza boy. They ran up the stairs, leaving Chloe alone in the entrance foyer.

Chloe couldn't explain why, but she felt a little relieved that the girls did not belong to Ethan. She looked for a spot to rest the heavy box of chocolates. The small hallway table was too narrow. French doors to her right and left were shut, and there didn't appear to be any activity behind them. Music and voices drifted down the staircase directly in front of her. She decided it was best to wait where she was and have Ernest lead her to the party.

She shifted her weight, balancing the box on one hip. She did a quick check in the mirror above the table, adjusting her foil candy-wrapper hair bow. She fidgeted with the bow and then glanced down to check out her jeweled slippers. How long did it take to pay a pizza boy?

When she looked up, Ed, followed by Ethan, descended the stairs. She took a second glance to make sure the man in the worn jeans with holes at the knees and ratty sweatshirt was really the Ethan Behar she knew. Of course it was. There was no mistaking that air of confidence and poise. Seeing him without a designer shirt or tailored pants was almost as intimate as if he wore nothing. She forced herself to look away. Ethan didn't need a polished veneer to attract her attention.

"Hey, where's the pizza? The girls said the pizza was here!" Ed shouted. When he noticed Chloe, he smiled and said, "You're not the pizza man."

"Sorry." She gave an innocent shrug.

"Chloe, what are you doing here?" Ethan missed a step but landed without mishap at the bottom of the staircase.

"Chocolate." Chloe wanted to kick herself for not having something more intelligent to say. "I'm delivering chocolates. Remember I bet you a box of my best that you couldn't find any Valrhona? I brought this for your mother's birthday." She was so embarrassed by the surprised look on Ethan's face, she almost let the box slip from her hands.

With an I'm-going-to-kill-you glare, she turned to Ed. "Here's your chocolate."

Ed walked over to her and put an arm around her shoulders. "I guess I forgot to mention to Big E that I invited you."

Chapter Ten

"What were you thinking, inviting her here?" Ethan raised his voice just enough to be heard above the chatter at the top of the stairs but not enough for Chloe to hear him. He was already trying to devise a plan that would get him out of this mess.

If he could somehow usher her out of there with an excuse that they had business to discuss, he doubted she would disagree. Ethan couldn't imagine that Chloe would want to be in the same room with him for such a long period of time. He was about to offer them both a way out, but it was too late.

"Hi, I'm Clare, Ethan's mother. You must be Chloe." When it came to Ethan and his brothers, their mother, Clare Behar, had a sixth sense. She gave them a warning look. "Ethan, why don't you and your brothers take the pizzas to the table. Everyone's starving."

Seeing the amusement in Chloe's eyes, Ethan laughed. "This is the only woman who can boss me around like that." He planted a kiss on his mother's forehead.

Chloe held out the box of chocolates. "These are for you. Happy birthday."

"What a lovely box," Clare said.

Ethan stood close enough to hear what his mother had to say to Chloe.

"You are even more adorable than Ed described." She raised her eyebrows and turned to Ethan. "I can't imagine why you kept her such a secret."

Ethan had not meant to glance in Chloe's direction, but he did so without thinking. Her soft, petite body provided a sharp contrast to his burly brothers, standing behind her.

She looked at him too, tilted her head, shrugged gently, and said mischievously, "Ethan *knows* secrets about me too."

His eyes immediately went to the spot where he had discovered her belly-button ring.

What had his mother said? *Adorable* wasn't quite the way he would describe Chloe. He smiled inwardly. Was that bow in her hair made from a candy wrapper? She wore a flaming red skirt and a little leather jacket, Tough but tender and sexy—that was Chloe. But he wasn't supposed to be thinking of her that way. She was nothing more than his latest business deal. And he would reinforce that point with his brothers once they were alone.

Ethan sensed that Ed was about to misinterpret the way he had glanced at Chloe. From his brother's perspective, it might appear that they were sharing an intimate greeting, but her comment, "Ethan knows secrets" had held that slight edge of defiance he had come to admire.

"Come on, dear, let me introduce you to the rest of the family." Clare began to move the group along just in time.

The Behar boys weren't moving, at least not until Ed added his two cents' worth. "Looks like this is going to be a very interesting evening."

"Not if I can help it." Ethan's gruff response got a chuckle from Ernest. Luckily, Chloe was out of hearing range.

The exchange did not go unnoticed by their mother. "The pizza is getting cold." She reached for Ethan's arm, almost upsetting the pizza boxes. "Make sure you and your brothers settle whatever it is that has you looking so sour before you join us."

It didn't take Ethan long to regroup his thoughts. He knew how to take the lead in negotiations, and dealing with his brothers was not much different. However, dealing with Chloe Brandeau was unlike any situation he had ever encountered. Maybe having her here would turn out to be a good thing. He could study her further, and she would get the opportunity to see that he was not a heartless monster eager to make a deal at her expense or to leave her homeless.

The pizza was devoured quickly. Chloe helped clear the table, carrying boxes and plates into the kitchen, where Ethan and Ed were finishing their beers and discussing the starting pitcher for the Yankees' opening game.

When Chloe entered, Ed announced he had to add the finishing touches to the birthday cake. "I think I'll let the kids put the whipped cream and berries on top." He balanced supplies in each hand and left the kitchen.

Ethan took the boxes from Chloe and placed them on the counter.

She looked past him, around the kitchen. "This is a nice layout."

"Up-to-date kitchens are a good investment for resale." He leaned casually against the counter. "My parents did a major renovation a few years ago. Ed helped them redesign the kitchen." He finished off his beer and reached for another. He took the first sip and thought how he should approach the delicate topic of her showing up there tonight. From the conversation at dinner, it was obvious that Ed had been very persuasive with all parties concerned. His family thought it was perfectly natural for Chloe to be there, and that was a dangerous situation for Ethan. His family life and his business were two separate entities, and he wanted to keep it that way.

Chloe Brandeau had somehow managed to upset the delicate balance he struggled to maintain. Still, standing in his parents' kitchen with her did seem natural.

"Ed did a nice job." Chloe slid her hand across the granite countertop, stopping just short of Ethan's side.

Ethan watched her hand move across the smooth granite. He was no longer thinking of renovations. He forgot what he wanted to say, concentrating instead on his quivering muscles. He imagined those slender, artistic fingers continuing on, touching him. What power did she have to make him feel this way? He couldn't blame the chocolate this time.

He was a man of action, but Ethan knew this situation was an opportunity he should let pass.

He stepped toward her, expecting her to jerk away. The uncertain look on her face made him hesitate only a brief moment before stepping closer still. When she didn't move, he slid his fingers down the length of her arm, capturing her hand. He pressed a kiss into her palm, testing her. Again, she didn't move away. Was she waiting for him to complete what he had started?

He had never backed away from something he

wanted. And he wanted her in his arms. From the first day he saw her, he'd thought about this moment. *Not a good idea,* his conscience warned.

The swinging door opened with a bang. "Oh, excuse me." Ed did an abrupt about-face and returned to the dining room.

Chloe jumped back, upsetting the empty pizza cartons.

His reflexes on high alert, Ethan caught the boxes before they hit the floor. Some crumbs, however, managed to escape.

Chloe stooped to sweep the crumbs onto a paper towel.

Ethan kneeled down beside her and tossed the towelful of crumbs into the sink. With his free hand, he helped her to her feet.

She looked up at him and said, "I never should have come here tonight."

"It wasn't my idea." His words were cruel, and he was instantly sorry he had said them.

"It's not part of your plan?"

"Plan? What plan?" Did she think he had connived with his brother to get her there tonight?

Before he could say anything else, Chloe forged ahead. "I don't want you to think that meeting your family and seeing you on a different playing field has changed anything. My little shop and run-down apartment building are as important to me as your multimillion-dollar deals are to you." She stepped back.

There was a seductive arrogance in her defiance. Something flared through him. He couldn't turn away from her. He wanted to pull her into his arms and finish what they had started. Instead he said, "I never meant to discredit what you do."

"Shouldn't we join the party?" She backed away.

He watched her brush a stray pink-tipped wisp of hair off her cheek. The simple gesture left him speechless.

She waited for his answer.

"Yeah. That's a good idea." Ethan followed her into the dining room. He held out a chair for her but did not take a seat. He stood against a wall. Convincing his brother that there was nothing romantic between him and Chloe would now be impossible. Even more important, could Ethan convince himself that this was nothing more than a primeval attraction? She had stimulated his senses with her kooky style and stubbornness.

There was a new arrival at the table. Brad, Ethan's driver, had joined the party. The Behars had known him since he was a kid, and even before Ethan had hired him as his driver, he was a familiar face at the Behar table. He left his seat and joined Ethan.

"Heard you were a little busy in the kitchen, boss."

"Who told you that?"

"When I got here, I was surprised you weren't out here, playing with the kids. Little E told me not to disturb you."

"I was in the kitchen."

"You weren't alone." Brad chuckled and glanced in Chloe's direction.

Ethan didn't want to watch her, but he found himself unable to take his eyes off of her. Once or twice she looked in his direction and caught him at his study. She simply smiled and turned away. Was she fidgeting with her napkin because she felt uneasy sitting at the table with his family? He couldn't blame her. It was quite possible that Ed had come out of the kitchen and announced to the family that he didn't believe a word of what Ethan had said about their relationship.

Clare put Chloe's chocolates on the table. "The box is so pretty, I almost hate to open it."

Everyone agreed, but that did not stop over-eager hands from grabbing the ends of the pink and brown bow. One gentle tug, and the bow flew off. His mother did the honors, slowly removing the lid. Everyone waited like kids at Christmas for a glimpse of what was inside.

Ethan had expected his nieces to react this way, but seeing grown people do it was mind-boggling. *Just for a piece of candy?* You would think they had never seen chocolate before.

"Now, that's a box of chocolates." The remark came from the last person Ethan had expected to react. His father reached for a dark-chocolate square.

"Wait." Clare tapped her husband's hand. "Let Chloe explain what's in each piece before we grab. I don't want you biting into these beautiful candies, not liking the center, and wasting any."

"What kind of candy do you usually like?" Chloe asked.

"Whatever I can get my hands on." The elder Mr. Behar looked up at Clare and smiled. "This old girl doesn't let me enjoy those simple pleasures too often."

Ethan was about to offer that his father's confection preferences were not fixed beyond anything more exotic than a Chunky, but Chloe was doing fine on her own.

"It's important to take small bites and let the flavors tease your taste buds." Chloe chose a creamy truffle. "I think you'll like this."

She was better than Ethan could ever have imagined. Simply standing in his parents' dinning room, without even the power of the Mayan bowls, she mesmerized his family. What had she used on him moments ago?

The entire family waited for Dad's reaction. He bit slowly into the candy, just as Chloe had instructed. "Wow. What was in that?"

"Vanilla custard."

Everyone around the table broke into a chorus of, "Pick one for me."

"Let it liquefy in your mouth to experience the textures on your palate," Chloe instructed. And she had the family literally eating out of her magical hand.

Ed came alongside him. "It's amazing, isn't it?"

Ethan didn't like being at odds with his brother, but he couldn't shake the annoyance that still lingered from Ed's meddling in something he had no understanding of. "I don't get it. They're acting like a bunch of kids let loose in Willy Wonka's factory."

"You're not too far off. Remember when we were kids?" Ed nudged him with an elbow. "Hard as it is to imagine, even you were a kid. Remember how difficult it was to decide which candy bar to buy?"

Ethan agreed. "I worked hard for my allowance. Picking out a candy bar was a major decision. Investing in a solid milk chocolate bar versus one with a gooey center was a difficult choice."

"It's always about money with you." Ed punched Ethan's shoulder. "Add a few decades, and chocolate still has the same appeal, only it's more sophisticated now."

"She's good, isn't she?" Ethan said.

"Better than good." Ed smiled and disappeared into the kitchen. When he returned, he held a cake piled high with layers of whipped cream, berries, and chocolate flakes.

His family responded to Ed's cake with the same sounds of pleasure they had made when Chloe's chocolates appeared.

Ethan wanted to join the happy group but knew he shouldn't. He needed to keep his distance from Chloe. It was time to get back on track and focus on the reason he was pursuing her. He needed her apartment building and nothing else. A moment of flirting in the kitchen had been just that and nothing more.

Ed bumped into him. "Hey, join the party. You can't stay back here and admire the view all night."

Reluctantly Ethan joined the group. His youngest niece begged for a horsey ride on his back. Grateful for the distraction, he obliged, bouncing her around the table.

"Uncle Ethan," she said, "if you marry Miss Chloe, will we get all the chocolate we want?"

Ethan imagined Chloe accompanying him to family events. His ex-wife had never been fond of Behar get-togethers. "Now where would you get such a silly idea? Miss Chloe and I are not getting married." Ethan glared at Ed, wondering exactly what he told the family after he walked into the kitchen.

Ed shrugged, feigning innocence.

Silence fell over the group. They glanced at Ethan and waited for his answer. He didn't want to, but he found himself looking for Chloe. How had she reacted to the comment?

Chloe appeared otherwise occupied, and he wondered if she had even heard the child's question. She busied herself rearranging the almost empty candy box.

"Oh, here it is." Chloe handed his niece of piece of foil-wrapped chocolate. "This one has a surprise inside."

The little girl slid off Ethan's back and eagerly ripped open her treat. "You'd better marry her," she told her uncle as she stuffed the candy into her mouth. Chocolate oozed around her lips. "May I have another one?"

Clare stepped in with a napkin. "I think we've all had enough chocolate and cake for one night."

"But I had only a half of piece of cake and one chocolate." She pointed to her sister and said, "She ate her whole piece of cake and candy too." Her hands rested on the hips of her pink tutu. "That's not fair."

Ethan offered an intervention. "How about you share this piece of candy with your sister?"

The Halloween princess looked at her grandmother with pleading eyes, willing to accept Ethan's terms.

"Everything is negotiable according to your Uncle Ethan." His mother cut the candy in half. She looked at Chloe and asked, "Don't you find that tiresome, dear?"

"Oh, you have no idea how annoying he can be,"

Chloe said, obviously enjoying the conversation. She glared at him across the table.

His mother was staring at them, looking slightly bemused. Nothing got past Clare Behar when her sons were involved. Ethan hoped she was beginning to see through this hoax Ed had created. It would make things easier when he told her the truth about their relationship. But he had never been more wrong.

"We all hope Chloe will visit us again," his mother announced.

"I'd love to, but I also hope you'll stop by my shop and visit me." She winked at the girls. "I'm working on a chocolate pizza."

"Chocolate pizza? Sounds interesting," Ethan's dad offered. "I'm coming even without the girls."

"It's still a work in progress. I'll send you one when I'm done."

Evidence of his family's infatuation was everywhere. Ethan didn't know how to put an end to it. If things continued at this pace, he too would melt deeper and deeper into the sticky cauldron of Chloe's charm.

Chloe put an end to the conversation when she stood to leave. "I can't thank you enough for letting me share in your celebration. But I have to get into my shop early, so I'm going to say good night." She smiled at Ethan too.

He tried to imagine what the evening would have been like without Chloe and her magical chocolates.

Against his better judgment, he knew that the combination had been the perfect birthday gift for his mother.

"It was our pleasure, dear." Clare kissed Chloe on the cheek, then asked, "How are you getting home?"

"The bus. It's still running." Chloe answered matter-of-factly.

Everyone around the table laughed, but Chloe looked confused. It was Mr. Behar who made it clear what everyone found so humorous. "She's a keeper, son. You've got a perfectly good vehicle and a chauffeur available, and this sweet little thing is going to take the bus?"

Brad tossed Ethan the keys. "You don't mind do you, boss? I haven't had my dessert yet."

Ethan caught the keys in midair and closed his fist around them. Everyone seemed out to annoy him tonight. Everyone except Chloe. She had worked her charm on him and his family. After this evening he knew for sure he wanted more than just her old building.

Chapter Eleven

Chloe wrestled with the age-old dilemma: Should she invite Ethan in or say good night at the curb? She considered her options. After all, she had seen a very different side to Ethan this evening. Tonight's Ethan could sit at her kitchen table. He might even allow himself to enjoy a cup of her hot cocoa. But what if the other Ethan surfaced, and he took her invitation as an opportunity to talk business? Would either Ethan even want to come in? Chloe stepped onto the curb, still not sure what to do.

Ethan had gotten out of the car too, and he looked up at the brick structure facing him. "This is a grand old building. I'll bet the inside has thick fire walls, crown moldings, and arched doorways."

Ethan had just described her apartment. Before moving in with her Aunt Bessie, Chloe had preferred more modern amenities, but she had come to appreciate the charm of these prewar buildings.

Interested in seeing the building from his point of view, she didn't object when he took her hand and directed her so that she was standing in front of him with her back toward him. His palms moved up her arms and rested on her shoulders. Leaning back, she trusted the contours of his body to support her. Her gaze followed the direction of his left hand.

"Look at the cornice projecting off the corner. It would be a challenge to preserve such a great example of Greek Revival architecture but well worth the effort."

Concentrating on the architecture was difficult as Ethan's right hand moved across her shoulder. He positioned her for a better view.

Chloe had never really taken a close look at the redbrick building. Most days she just rushed in and out of the front door. But tonight everything seemed to take on a new meaning.

"This building has only four floors," he continued. "Imagine it twice as high." Ethan spoke about Aunt Bessie's building with a passion that made it seem alive. "I can visualize a setback for the additional floors."

"A setback?"

"Each of the additional floors could be stacked in a way that would set it back from the floor below."

"It sounds so simple." Chloe tilted her head and looked at the roof from a different angle. It seemed perfectly natural to rest her head against his chest. "Kind of like stacking a tiered cake." She had always known the building had character, but she had believed it came from her aunt and her kooky tenants.

"It's a simple idea, but the process is pretty involved." His hands moved along her arms, gently caressing. "First you have to get permission to use the airspace."

"Airspace?" She found herself caught up not only in his enthusiasm, but also in the delicious movement of his thumb along her neck.

"The city has laws that prevent new buildings from blocking sunlight to the street and neighboring structures."

"What would you do with the existing floors?" Her skin tingled from the touch of his finger, but something else had sparked her interest. She wanted to hear more about his plans. Would he be interested in her ideas? Most important, she needed to know his intentions for the tenants who currently occupied the building.

"I would have the architects preserve what's already there. Most of the original apartments would remain intact, with modern upgrades."

"Could you find a way to let the current tenants stay where they are?" Chloe swung around to face him. "Without a rent increase?"

He looked down at her and smiled, put his arms around her, and drew her toward him. "Chloe, you never fail to amaze me."

Her heart pounded from his closeness and her anticipation of his answer.

It had probably been unfair to ask him such a loaded question. Perhaps he needed to see more of the building. "Want to see what the place looks like from the inside?" Inviting him in suddenly seemed like the right thing to do. She withdrew from his arms and walked backward to the front of the building.

Ethan surprised her when he hesitated. "It's getting late."

"You may never get another chance." Chloe knew she had just offered him the best piece of chocolate in the box, but most likely he feared the consequences of accepting it.

"If I owned this place, it'd be the most sought-after piece of real estate in the neighborhood." His voice sounded far away.

"It already is." She couldn't resist teasing him about his own persistence. "Aren't you interested?"

"I'm very interested." He reached for her hand.

Chloe understood he was no longer talking real estate. She felt a thrill at the prospect of what Ethan was really interested in. And she wanted him to kiss her. Pushing the thought from her mind, she pulled her hand from his. There would be no deals or anything else tonight. Things were happening much too fast. Just a quick tour of her apartment was all she was offering.

She led the way, and Ethan followed.

Inside her apartment, a horrid stench assaulted her sensitive sense of smell. If Ethan noticed, he didn't comment, or maybe he was too busy exploring the width of the walls and height of the ceiling.

Chloe rushed off to open the kitchen window. The room smelled like a compost heap. She looked around and found the culprit in her kitchen sink. Someone's dinner scraps gurgled up from the drain.

"Smells like a plumbing problem." Ethan stood in the doorway.

"Just a little backup. Want to see the rest of the place?" She urged him back into the living room. "I'll call Henry in the morning."

Ethan gripped her shoulders and turned her around. "Can't let you spend the night with this stink. Let me take a look."

She would have laughed if the smell wasn't so overwhelming.

Before she knew it, Ethan was under her sink, banging on the pipes and mumbling something about a wrench and a bucket.

She found a wrench in a toolbox stashed away with Aunt Bessie's relics. An old stainless steel mixing bowl took the place of a bucket.

"You sure you know what you're doing?"

"Hey, don't worry." Ethan wriggled out from under the sink. He took the wrench and turned its wheel. "I learned how to use one of these before I could walk." He slid back under the sink.

Chloe stooped down to offer her help. It was too dark to see much. "I've got a flashlight."

"Darn it. Too late for that."

Chloe looked down the sink drain and saw a small portion of Ethan's face. From what she could see of him, he wasn't too happy.

She squatted down beside the cabinet door. "Maybe you should come out of there."

"You've got everyone's dinner scraps backed up into your pipes." He handed her the wrench, now covered with sludge.

"Ugh." She took it with her fingertips and, without thinking, tossed it into the sink. It landed with a loud clang against the stainless steel basin, leaving a streak of grease in her shiny sink. She turned on the water. "Oh, no!" Chloe gasped when she realized what she had done. "I'm so sorry."

Ethan emerged from under the sink. Sitting on her kitchen floor, wet, covered with wilted salad and some other unrecognizable sludge, Ethan Behar looked nothing like the man who had come to her shop the day Henry the Hot Dog fell down.

That *GQ* man was not her type—too perfect and confident. Now he looked more like a piece of candy melting on a hot sidewalk than a real-estate tycoon.

Under all the slime he still managed to laugh. "I guess I've lost my knack for this kind of thing."

"Is it possible that I've just witnessed your first failure?" She reached for a paper towel and wiped a smudge off his forehead. "Don't tell me you were once a plumber." Her stomach fluttered, but not from the mess covering him. Being so close to him sent her heart racing as well.

"Not a licensed plumber, but I used to know how to handle a wrench. When I was sixteen, I worked for a neighbor who owned a small apartment building similar to this." He put his hand over hers, guiding her as she wiped lettuce off his face. "I did odd jobs—painting, roof repairs, and some basic plumbing."

The goo was gone, but he didn't release her hand. She swallowed hard and imagined he wanted to kiss her, but he didn't. Her mind told her that this was wrong and would lead to trouble, but her body refused to move. She watched his mouth move and admired the long, classic line of his jaw as he continued talking, edging closer with each word.

"My brothers and I would ride around the neighborhood, and they'd kid me because I was always asking what they would build on the empty lots."

"What did they say?"

"They never had an answer."

"But you did." She studied his face, wondering what had made him so determined.

"Absolutely." His eyes met hers, and she felt her heart skip a beat.

She took a deep breath, hoping for a hint of his clean, masculine scent. Tonight his usually wonderful aftershave was overpowered by the stench, however, reminding her that they couldn't sit forever on the messy floor. "You need a shower. I'll get some more paper towels."

He stopped her, took the paper towel, and tossed it aside. In one sweeping motion she was in his arms. "Why don't I get you all dirty too, and we can clean up together?"

The scene at his parents' house had been merely a tease. This time he didn't hesitate. He kissed her with a heated passion that left her breathless. Without looking away, she twisted in his arms, pulling away, denying the passion she saw in his eyes and the desire rising in her like a pot of chocolate ready to boil.

"The bathroom is the second door on the left." Chloe backed away and pointed down the narrow hallway. "There are towels under the sink."

It was impossible not to be attracted to him. The man was a single girl's dream: successful, good genes, and handy with pipes and wrenches. But she and he were as different as a bag of M&Ms and Valrhona chocolate. He rode in chauffeured vehicles. She took the bus. He wore expensive designer clothes. She had a closetful of thrift-store bargains.

Stolen kisses in a kitchen were not what she wanted from a relationship. The lingering thought that Ethan was doing all this to get her building still sat in the back of her mind. She had to end this nonsense before they both went too far to go back.

When Chloe heard the shower whistling, she felt more comfortable going into her bedroom to find a T-shirt suitable for Ethan. She got as far as the living room when she heard a loud pounding on the door.

"Chloe, Chloe. It's me, Sadie Katz."

The porcelain clock on the dusty end table read 11:15. What did Sadie want? Could the backed-up pipes be affecting her apartment too?

Chloe unlocked the dead bolt and chain. Sadie was not alone. Mr. Liang and the tenant from 4C stood outside her door.

"We were playing mahjong and heard a terrible banging in the pipes." Sadie stepped past the open door. "There's not going to be a problem again, is there?"

"Oh, no. Everything is taken care of. I had a little backup in my drain, but it's fine now."

"Are you sure?" Sadie glanced over Chloe's shoulder. "Since we're all up and here in your apartment, why don't you fix us a cup of your delicious hot cocoa?" Sadie started to lead the way to the kitchen but stopped when Ethan appeared at the bathroom door.

"What's that man doing here at this hour?" Sadie asked.

"Fixing the pipes," Ethan offered. "Everything's under control now. Thanks for stopping in."

Sadie was not so easily dismissed and pushed past Chloe for a better look at Ethan.

Chloe lowered her head into her hands, but not without first seeing Ethan standing half-naked under the living room arch. He was bare-chested, with his worn jeans loosely belted at the waist.

"Maybe it wasn't the pipes that we heard making all that noise." Mr. Liang winked at Chloe.

"It was the pipes. The pipe in my kitchen sink." Chloe, afraid that her thoughts had become obvious, felt her skin turn candy-apple red. She tried to explain, unsure if she could without exposing her confusing relationship with Ethan. "He fixed the pipe." She pointed over her shoulder to avoid looking at Ethan. "The lettuce and all that stuff got all over him, so he took a shower."

Blank faces stared at her as she rattled on. Finally, at a loss for a better explanation, she turned to Ethan for help. His wet hair dripped onto his bare chest, and her breath caught in her throat.

Ethan didn't have anything to add. Chloe fell back on her usual solution at a time like this. "Hot chocolate sounds great. Sadie, please set up the pot while I find Ethan a shirt. You can use the molinillo my parents sent from Mexico."

"Everyone into the kitchen." It was Mr. Liang who ushered the mahjong players out of the room.

Chloe realized that inviting Ethan to see her apartment had been her biggest mistake of the day. He had seemed so sincere and genuinely interested in the building as an entity and not as an acquisition. Had she read him wrong? But what did he really have to gain from seeing the inside of her apartment? She didn't want to believe it simply was another of his tactics.

"You could have said something, anything, to help me out," she said to him. What was it about this man? From the day of their first meeting, whenever he showed up, situations seemed to go from bad to worse.

"Mrs. Katz and I don't seem to meet under the best of circumstances. Do you always have such curious, unexpected guests?" A sly smile curled Ethan's lips. He seemed to find the late-night visitors amusing. "What's a molinillo?" He rubbed a cotton-candypink towel over his head, then hung it around his neck.

"It's a twisted wooden stick."

"What's Sadie going to do with it?" He faked a shudder.

"It's like a whisk, used for frothing hot chocolate." Chloe yanked her towel off his shoulders. "Don't move until I come back with a shirt," she warned.

Ethan didn't listen. He followed her and stood in the bedroom doorway, distracting her from her task.

She went into her closet and rummaged through a basket of oversized T-shirts. When she found one she thought would be suitable, she tossed it to Ethan and said, "This should fit."

"I don't think it's quite my color." Ethan studied the orange Grateful Dead shirt before slipping it over his head.

Chloe giggled. She had to agree, burnt orange was not the most flattering color she had seen him wear. "It will have to do. You can't go driving around half-dressed. Imagine what the headlines would say if someone saw you."

"It wouldn't be the first time I've gotten bad press." He glanced over his shoulder. "Want me to stay and help out with the mahjong group?"

"I don't think that's a very good idea. You don't even like my hot chocolate."

"I'm acquiring an unquenchable thirst." He kissed the top of her head and slipped quietly by the kitchen door.

Chapter Twelve

"You can't imagine the ruckus you've created." Sarah stood at the display counter and watched Chloe layer trays with dark and light chocolate.

Chloe didn't need to be reminded that Sadie and her mahjong players were better than the *Daily News'* morning edition. She reached for a stray truffle, but Sarah got to it first.

Sarah waited before tasting the decadent candy. She still had plenty more to say. "Every one of my clients along Atlantic Avenue had only one topic on their mind today." She glanced at Chloe with an is-there-anything-you-want-to-tell-me look. "They all wanted to hear about you and Ethan Behar."

Chloe shook her head, still preferring not to comment. She busied herself rearranging the tray of chocolates.

"I wouldn't worry about it." Henry, dressed in his ice-cream-sundae suit, had met Sarah on the street. "I'll have one of those." He reached for a candy and popped it into his mouth. "Sounds like Ethan is interested in more than Chloe's building."

Chloe had had about as much as she was going to take. Sarah and Henry were not the first to ask her about the events of the past evening. Several of her early-morning deliverymen had heard about her and Ethan from their other customers.

"The garbageman, the mailman, everyone insinuated I had let them down, consorted with the enemy." Chloe walked away from the counter, trying to ignore her friends. The evening hadn't been about Ethan's taking her home. So much more had happened.

Sarah followed. "Maybe they see you as their last chance to stand up to the developers."

Chloe was no fool. She knew exactly what Ethan represented, but she had also seen another side of him. She hadn't digested all the events of the previous evening or what it meant to their relationship. If she even had a relationship with him. Whatever it was, she wasn't about to share it with her friends. Not just yet.

Surprisingly, she had liked Ethan's family. Memories of her own childhood had surfaced last night. Being an only child of parents with a weird passion for digging up dirt and rocks, she had gravitated toward friends from large families with normal jobs. Ethan's family fit all those criteria, except being Ethan's friend was the furthest thing from her mind.

She wasn't so sure how he felt about her. The one thing she would bet on was that he was still interested in acquiring her building. She wanted to believe that the passion she had seen in his eyes was sincere, but she still had a nagging suspicion that he was simply trying to seduce her with his charm. It was all a game to him, no matter what he considered the prize. Once again, he was the cause of this morning's gossip. The more Chloe thought about it, the madder she got.

"That's how he operates," she retorted. "I know. I read an article about him."

"You and that article. You've been up close and personal with the most eligible bachelor in the city, and you're still quoting from some stuffy article." Sarah gave her a questioning glance. "Is this just a cover for your real feelings for him?"

"No way," Chloe lied. She preferred thinking of Ethan as an entity that reporters wrote about; it reminded her why he was pursuing her in the first place. The real Ethan Behar had a different impact on her psyche, and she wasn't sure she could handle that.

"It's hard to imagine someone of Ethan's status

getting covered with sink sludge for just any pretty face." Sarah handed Henry a candy and popped another into her mouth. "I told you to give him my card. I could set him up as your next date."

"Absolutely not. That would finish off our deal with a bang." Chloe slammed the tray forcefully onto the counter. The truffles jiggled across the shiny metal, settling in a corner and upsetting her perfect arrangement.

"Which deal—the one you and I have, or the deal Ethan is trying to close?" Sarah asked.

The question unsettled Chloe. How could she answer her friend without admitting her feelings for the conniving master of acquisitions? He was good. He had assessed her goals and resources and found her vulnerable.

"You're in desperate need of an intervention. You still want a date for the Chocolate Ball?"

"It would be nice not to go alone this year." Chloe glanced at Henry. He looked more appetizing as a sundae than he did as a hot dog. "What are you doing June twelfth?" she asked him.

Henry finished chewing before he answered. "Sorry, I'm busy that day. Sarah asked me to accompany her to her cousin's wedding."

"Oh?" Chloe looked at her friend. Was Sarah blushing? At least someone had made a pudding out of this whole melted mess. "Who would have thought that my hot dog and my matchmaker would find each other?"

Henry was a nice guy. Some people might think Chloe had made a big mistake by not pursuing a relationship with him. His handyman business seemed to be taking off after word got out that he had repaired her ancient, leaky pipes.

Was she being too picky? She looked at the way he seemed so natural inside his ice-cream costume. He was definitely the type of guy who would be okay using one of those baby-carrier things. Should she have considered Henry? Some people might consider Mr. Swifter a better catch. Chloe shuddered. She never settled for second best, and she wasn't about to do so now. If she settled, she might miss out on meeting her true soul mate.

After last night, she realized that a big part of her problem was her limited exposure to socializing normally with other people. Even the infamous Ethan Behar had a family life to balance his hectic schedule. Who would have imagined that the hard-nosed wheeler-dealer knew how to give a six-year-old a piggyback ride? And even more astonishing, he'd seemed to enjoy it.

Sarah adjusted the cherry on top of Henry's head. "There are a few potential clients I'm considering for your next date."

"I have faith you'll come through with date number

three just like you promised." Chloe rolled her eyes. After the events of the last few weeks, she considered ending the agreement with Sarah. She could go alone to the ball. But maybe Sarah was right. Dating more men might prevent her from making the wrong decision.

Chloe never felt the panic or desperation some unattached thirty-somethings felt when there was no sign of their true love arriving at their doorstep. Yet for a brief moment last night she had believed she might be on her way to finding that dream man.

"Maybe we should go beyond the three-date agreement," Chloe said impulsively.

Sarah paused with a candy at her lips. "Did you just say what I thought you said?"

"Playing the field may not be such a bad idea. I wouldn't want to miss out on the perfect situation." Chloe forced a laugh. "Or the perfect man."

"So, you're game for whatever I plan?" Sarah did a little victory dance.

Chloe glanced at the Mayan bowls. "Sure, fine, whatever. It's a masked ball, so if he has a third eye, it won't matter." She gave Henry an apologetic look.

Henry was preoccupied with his headgear. He disregarded Chloe's comment with a shrug.

"Okay, so a third eye is acceptable." Sarah scribbled on the back of an old receipt. "Any other considerations?"

"I'll leave it up to you. Isn't that what I pay you for?"

"Pay me?" Sarah covered her mouth and tried to hide the evidence of the second piece of chocolate she'd filched.

Chloe pointed to the disarranged tray of chocolates. "At twenty-one dollars a pound, you're eating the profits now."

"Okay, I get your point. I know I eat my share of candy every time I come in. I do the same when I visit Mike and Alex at the cupcake store."

"You work on getting me a date. I've got to concentrate on putting together my chocolate pizza for the big event." Chloe hoped Sarah would accept her answer and end the conversation.

Defining their roles was just the topic her friend needed to change the subject. "Weren't you planning on entering some kind of chocolate-covered cherry?"

"I was. I planned to soak an entire cherry, stem included, in a cherry cordial and let it marinate for weeks." Chloe released a lone, exasperated sigh. "Imagine taking your first bite—the cordial, the fruit, and delicious chocolate." She leaned back against the wall, careful not to dislodge the Mayan bowls. Images of delicate chocolate-covered cherries floated through her mind. "Oh, well, there's always next year."

"They sound wonderful, almost too much for one person to handle." Sarah gripped the counter for support. "Why aren't you entering them?"

"Life seemed to get ahead of me this year. I missed out on cherry season."

"At least pizza's not seasonal. How's the chocolate pizza going?" Henry asked.

"Not well." Chloe replied. "Marzipan coated with white chocolate turned out to be the perfect solution for the pizza dough, but the red glaze looked more like a melted candy apple than tomato sauce."

"Can you add something to the glaze?" Henry pointed to the fuzzy fabric hanging off the sides of his sundae suit.

Chloe thought for a moment, closing her eyes as she tried to picture Henry's suggestion. "Henry, you're a chocolate genius!" She planted a kiss on his cheek. "I could add a white drizzle. It would look like cheese and dull the shine of the glaze. What would I do without the two of you?"

"Have more chocolate to sell." Henry reached for another truffle.

The door opened, and Chloe turned her attention to what she thought was her next paying customer.

"Good afternoon, Miss Brandeau."

She had seen this man once before. He was a representative from Ethan's office. Then she remembered his last visit. He was the baggy-pants accountant who had sampled her most expensive chocolate.

Chloe took the tray of truffles and hid them under

the counter. She glanced at his card. ROGER FLYNN, CPA. "What can I do for you, Mr. Flynn?"

"May I speak to you in private?" Mr. Baggy Pants asked.

"These are my friends. Whatever you have to say can be said in front of them."

"I'm here to make you an offer." He opened his attaché case and removed a pile of official-looking papers. "I've seen the contract, and it's a more than generous offer, considering the condition of your building."

"What do you know about the condition of my building?"

"My employer has an extensive research department. You can be assured he knew everything there was to know before he had this new offer prepared."

"I've heard about his research department." Chloe took the sealed envelope. It was a standard business envelope with Ethan Behar's letterhead in the corner. "Why isn't he here with the offer?"

"He had urgent matters to attend to today."

"I'll bet." Chloe remembered the urgency of his kiss. Was Ethan being cautious? Had her question about letting her tenants stay disturbed him?

Sarah stepped forward. "An offer?"

"And you are . . . ?" Roger asked over the rim of his glasses.

"I'm her accountant." Sarah switched roles without even blinking. She took the envelope and gave Chloe a should-I-open-it look.

Roger looked to Chloe for confirmation before addressing Sarah again. "Yes, an offer from Mr. Behar. He's still interested in your client's apartment building."

"Among other things," Henry mumbled.

Chloe was having second thoughts about allowing her friends to stay. Well, at least they would witness firsthand and be able to confirm that she had been right about Ethan all along. He was a wheeler-dealer who would use whatever tactics he could to complete his deal. Even something as special as kissing her senseless and making her believe he enjoyed it too.

"I haven't changed my mind." Chloe tried to take the envelope from Sarah, but she resisted.

"At least take a look inside," Sarah suggested.

"No." Chloe jerked the papers from her friend. Without even glancing at them, she handed them to Roger. "Your boss and I discussed options other than money. Would you know if he added any of those details to the new contract?"

Roger shook his head. "Everything stays the same, but the new offer is for an obscene amount of cash."

"Money isn't everything." Chloe reached for her chocolate pot. She gave her friends a warning look. "At least not to me." She wrapped her fingers around the pot while she studied the man Ethan had sent to do his bidding. He seemed pleasant enough; it wasn't his fault his boss was a creep.

"I hate to see your trip down here be for nothing. Would you like a hot cocoa?"

She tried not to think about how her life as a simple chocolate maker had gotten so complicated. Instead she began to imagine what she would say to Ethan if she ever saw him again. *I always have men covered with sludge sitting on my kitchen floor, and of course I kiss them whenever I get the chance. Why did I ever agree to spend an evening with your family in the first place? A moment of temporary insanity is my only explanation.*

What she wouldn't tell him was how her heart beat faster when he touched her or how much she enjoyed the newly-discovered side of him. She stopped herself. She wasn't going to spend another second thinking about Ethan.

"Do you like your cocoa with marshmallows or whipped cream?" She watched the half-extracted papers being stuffed back into their envelope.

"I prefer whipped cream, but I have my orders." Mr. Baggy Pants tried to flash an impersonal smile, but his mouth twitched. "Absolutely no hanging out, and definitely no sampling your wonderful chocolates."

Wonderful chocolates. Chloe felt as if she had just

been given a free-admission ticket. "It would be a crime to leave without at least buying some chocolates for your wife." If she could get this man to talk, she might find out what else Ethan had planned.

"I don't have a wife."

"You don't?" Sarah put her hands on Chloe's shoulders, sliding her to one side. "Do you have a girlfriend?"

"Not at the moment."

"Maybe I can help you out." Sarah ignored Chloe's warning glare. "Here's my card."

"I thought you said you were her accountant."

"I do a little dating-consulting on the side." She smiled. "Everyone here has been my client at one time or another."

"Everyone?" His eyes focused on Chloe, who now slipped behind Sarah.

"Yes, Chloe and Henry met on a date I arranged, and now they're the best of friends."

"Interesting." Roger tucked the card into the pocket of his tweed sport coat. "This is a most unusual place. I wish I could stay and enjoy some of your candy, but duty calls." He smiled at Chloe. "You really should reconsider this offer." He hesitated before tucking the envelope back into his attaché case. "Can't I at least convince you to read the contract before you make any hasty decisions?"

"I'm not interested in anything Ethan Behar has to offer." Chloe did not return his smile.

When the doorbell signaled he was gone, Sarah studied the card he had given Chloe. "What a weird little man. But he seemed to like you. He must be brilliant or something, because he definitely does not reflect your Ethan's style."

"*My* Ethan? I don't think so. You heard the man in the funny pants; he was forbidden to taste anything in this shop." Annoyed at herself for being so affected by the idea of Ethan's dictating what someone could or could not purchase in her shop, Chloe redirected her anger and snapped at her friend.

Turning her attention to some streaks on the counter, she rubbed it vigorously. She glanced up briefly to offer a faint good-bye when Henry squeezed his wide sundae through the door to leave.

Sarah did not leave with Henry. She stood directly in front of the counter, drumming her fingers on the spotless glass. "So, what do you think?" she asked.

Chloe tossed the paper towel into the trash. "What do I think about what?"

"Exactly what I thought. You're angry because Ethan's avoiding you."

"He's not avoiding me. You have to have some kind of relationship for someone to avoid you. One kiss does not link you to a person forever."

"He kissed you?" Sarah's mouth dropped open. She propped her elbows on the counter, leaning closer to Chloe. "And then what?"

"And then nothing. He fixed my sink." Chloe pointed to her clean counter. Sarah took the hint and backed away. "And let me refresh your memory. The sink is part of the building he's interested in buying. Did you already forget Mr. Baggy Pants the account-ant? It had nothing to do with me and everything to do with my apartment building."

"He didn't kiss the kitchen sink, did he?"

Chloe resisted the urge to roll her eyes in response to Sarah's question. Instead she looked away, afraid her friend would see from her expression how she re-ally felt about Ethan. He was exactly the kind of man she was looking for.

Chapter Thirteen

Ethan stood at the window of his DUMBO office. An article in *Architectural Interest* described this Brooklyn building as *industrial chic Down Under the Manhattan Bridge Overpass*. The building, one of his recent projects, already had a waiting list for completed office space. Lately he did his best thinking from this spot overlooking the New York City sky line. The most sensational morning view of the city was across the river to the west. He usually concentrated on the rooftops of Manhattan, admiring the assorted architectural styles. This morning his thoughts were preoccupied by what was going on in a certain chocolate shop on Union Street.

After leaving Chloe last night, he realized that it

would be best to close the deal and move on. The acquisition of her apartment building was crucial to the completion of the Butler Street project. He had already taken too long to resolve the matter standing in his way.

Getting involved personally had proven to be a disaster. He couldn't let his feelings for Chloe interfere with his deal any longer. Hard as he tried, he found it difficult to separate the two. His growing attraction to her had become a distraction from his main goal. Too many people depended on him to close this deal. The time had come to push his personal feelings aside and move forward.

There were other options to consider. He had already sent a memo to his architects, requesting a plan to add floors to Chloe's building. She had seemed interested in the design, and he might be able to use that to his advantage. First she had to agree to sell him her building. The increased offer should be hard to resist.

Once she signed on the dotted line, building up would be his first choice. The additional floors would house state-of-the-art condos.

To help him understand Chloe's loyalty to the tenants, Ethan checked into her Aunt Bessie, the previous owner's, background. He came up with an interesting bit of information. Aunt Bessie had a son, Allen, a prominent lawyer, who for some unexplained reason had not inherited his mother's apartment building. Ethan had attempted to call Allen, hoping he might offer some insight into Chloe's resistance to the sale. But Allen was out of the country, leaving Ethan to figure out for himself why Chloe was being so stubborn.

Behind him the door opened. When he turned, Roger Flynn stood in the doorway, an exasperated expression knitting his brow.

Ethan could only imagine what Chloe must have put the poor guy through. "Did she accept the deal?" He needed to know the building was his before he continued with his plans.

Roger tossed the envelope onto Ethan's desk. "I couldn't even get her to look inside."

"Did you at least tell her the amount?"

"I tried to, but she wouldn't listen. She asked about some new terms the two of you had discussed."

"I wouldn't call it a discussion. She has some crazy notion that I might let her current tenants stay." Ethan smiled, remembering how she'd fit into the contours of his body as they discussed his plans to maintain the existing architecture. He quickly dismissed the thought. He laughed. "And she doesn't want a rent increase."

"Oh, you didn't mention that part of your conversation." Roger adjusted his glasses. "You might want to consider some negotiation to include the tenants."

"Why?"

"Because you might not get this deal closed if you

don't. It depends on how important this building is to your project."

"You know it's the entire block or nothing." Ethan had never lost track of his main goal. "There's just one obstacle in the way."

"The apartment building?" Roger asked.

"No. The little lady who owns it." Ethan had a fair business relationship with all his employees. With Brad and Roger it was friendship too. They had been with him since the beginning. He had a feeling there was something Roger wanted to add. "What's bothering you?" he asked.

"I don't think she likes you very much."

"I don't give a damn if she likes me or not," Ethan lied. He did care. He had no intention of hurting her, which was why he had offered such an obscene amount of money. He had been more than generous. "She could buy a new building with working plumbing and take all her crazy tenants with her."

"Where?" Roger cleared his throat. "Where would she move?"

"How do I know where she'd move them?"

"That's the point, Ethan. Those people have lived in that neighborhood for so long, they don't want to move."

"What?" Ethan couldn't believe what he was hearing from his accountant. He had never known the man to give way under pressure. "I had a feeling she'd be difficult." He walked back to the window and pointed to the skyline. He had come across a similar problem with a property in Red Hook, but in the end the money was too good to pass up. "Thousands of buildings in this city, and I had to choose the one belonging to Chloe Brandeau." Finding solutions to difficult acquisitions was what he did best, but "solving" Chloe was not going to be easy. "I would still have to renovate those old apartments, and we'd have to relocate everyone in the process."

"I don't think she's going to cooperate." Roger shook his head to enhance his point. "Her tenants aren't interested in signature services or fancy apartments or a concierge in the lobby."

"You think they'd object to working plumbing?" Ethan's irritation deepened. He should have handled the deal himself.

Roger shrugged.

"You're not taking her side because she fed you some of her chocolate, are you?" Ethan looked suspiciously at Roger. If anyone understood how difficult it was to resist the sexy chocolatier, it was Ethan. He even imagined what it would be like if they had met under different circumstances and her apartment building was not standing between them.

"You said no chocolate. It was tough, but I resisted."

Ethan put an arm around Roger's shoulders. "C'mon, I'll buy you breakfast."

"I'm going to have to pass today. There's something I want to check into."

"Anything I can help you with?" Ethan asked.

Roger pulled out a business card. He handed it to Ethan and asked, "Have you ever used a dating service?"

Ethan gave his baggy-pants-wearing accountant a sly look. "You want to set me up with someone?"

"Oh, no. It's not for you. I was thinking of giving this Sarah a call for me."

"Sarah?" Ethan hadn't forgotten what Henry had told him. Chloe still had one more date to complete her agreement with Sarah. "Any of Sarah's clients in particular you're interested in dating?" Ethan had no claims on Chloe, but he had a strong suspicion where this conversation was heading.

"Chloe is one of her clients. Did you know that she set her up with a guy who dresses like an ice cream sundae?" Roger asked.

"Henry? I met him, but he was a hot dog when he dated Chloe." Ethan noticed the puzzled look on Roger's face. "He was the guy Brad and I drove to the ER a few weeks ago."

"I'm going to assume Chloe and Henry didn't work out."

Roger's questions were beginning to annoy Ethan.

"They're friends." There was no reason to share the information he had learned regarding Sarah and Chloe's matchmaking agreement.

"She's definitely one interesting little lady. Must be full of surprises on a date."

"You'd have to ask Henry."

"I'd like to find out for myself. I might give this matchmaker a call." Roger studied the card, then glanced at Ethan. "Unless you think it's a conflict of interest."

"Of course it's a conflict of interest." Ethan didn't feel any better knowing that his conservative accountant had been taken in by Chloe's charm. Roger was right on target. Being with Chloe was an endless, whirling, chocolatey swirl.

"Is there something going on between you and the Chocolate Lady?" Roger held out the card. He raised a suspicious eyebrow and asked, "Is there, boss?"

Ethan snapped the business card out of his hand and tucked it into his jacket pocket. "You know I don't eat chocolate and tell."

If Ethan wasn't so irritated, he might even laugh at the bizarre experiences he had whenever Chloe was around. Who would believe that a deal-closer like himself would be more concerned about a bleeding hot dog or missing chocolate bunnies than he would be in getting her signature on the bottom line?

Roger motioned that he was leaving. Ethan had no

reason to detain him. He preferred to be alone at the moment.

He returned to his position at the window. This time he wasn't studying the skyline. He took the business card he had snatched from Roger out of his pocket. Sending Roger to Chloe's shop with the contract had been a mistake, but time and choices were limited.

Ethan needed to reset his thinking. He couldn't avoid Chloe forever if he expected to close the deal to everyone's satisfaction. Even if and when he did manage to close the deal, he wasn't so sure he could just walk away and feel as if he had gotten everything he wanted.

Ethan stared at Sarah's card for several minutes before walking to his desk. What was it Henry had said—three dates with the objective of finding Chloe a date for her Chocolate Ball? He placed a hand on the phone but didn't pick it up. He had to be crazy to do what he was thinking, but the idea of someone else taking Chloe to the Chocolate Ball made him even crazier.

"Hello, you have reached Sarah. Your call is important, so please leave a message. I'll call you back as soon as possible. Thank you."

The beep sounded, and Ethan wasn't sure what kind of message he should leave. He left his name and office number, then called his secretary. "I'm expecting an important call from a woman named Sarah. Put the call right through."

He glanced at his watch, shuffled some papers, and stared at a blueprint of the ironworks building. He was about to leave the office when his phone rang.

"Mr. Behar, this is Sarah. I'm returning your call."

The ball was in Ethan's court. "I've come across a business card for your dating-consultant services. There's a specific client of yours I'm interested in having you arrange a date for me with." What was he doing? He was speaking to a matchmaker, not a business associate. "What I mean is, there is a certain one of your clients I'd like to date."

"I think we both know the lady you're talking about." Sarah didn't ask him to elaborate. "You can count on my discretion in this matter."

"Thank you. You'll make all the arrangements and phone my secretary with the information?" If he looked at this as a business arrangement, he might be able remain detached and keep his feelings under control—get Chloe to listen to his ideas and accept his new offer. He tried hard to convince himself that that was all he wanted.

"I can give you the information right now. Do you have a tux?" Had she just giggled? "Of course you do." In a more serious tone she asked, "Are you free next Saturday?"

Ethan didn't want to seem too eager. He hesitated,

picked up his BlackBerry, and checked his appointments. It was not unusual for him to have a meeting scheduled for a Saturday night. Next Saturday he was free, but he would have rearranged his schedule if necessary.

"Saturday will be fine."

"Great. There's a black-tie event at the Brooklyn Museum. It's a Chocolate Ball and contest being held in conjunction with their Mayan exhibit."

Was the whole world chocolate crazy? A Mayan exhibit and a Chocolate Ball? But he couldn't back out now.

"Mr. Behar, are you still there?"

"Yes. What time should I pick up my date?"

"Oh, no. You'll meet her there. And, by the way, it's a masked ball."

"A masked ball?" Ethan had been to masked affairs and knew that the disguises gave guests a license to behave somewhat out of character.

"Don't worry. The lady will be easy to spot."

"I'm sure she will be." Ethan imagined that the pink spikes of Chloe's hair would be visible over the top of her mask. "I see there's a fee for your service. I'll transfer you to my secretary, so you can get the information needed to send my bill."

Ethan transferred the call. Arranging the date with Chloe had been easier than he'd expected. It was almost as if Sarah had been expecting his call. So why was there a throbbing pain edging across his forehead? What had he been thinking when he made the call? The problem was, he wasn't thinking. He had let Roger's interest in Chloe affect his decision-making.

All was not lost, though. Ethan would use the occasion to his advantage and talk up his new plan for Chloe's building. Letting the current tenants stay was going to be difficult to maneuver around, but it might prove to be the only solution to closing the deal.

It wasn't like Ethan to second-guess himself, but a lot could happen before Saturday. He called Brad and told him to have the car waiting. He decided to pay a casual visit to Chloe's shop and see for himself if she had developed a strong animosity to him overnight.

On the ride to the Chocolate Boutique, Brad and Ethan kept the conversation to sports, avoiding any mention of Ethan's sudden craving for a certain chocolatier.

Union Street was busy with the afternoon lunch crowd when the black SUV pulled up in front of the store. Ethan thought nothing of the Mr. Swifter truck parked across the street until he spotted Phil coming out of Chloe's shop.

"Hey, Ethan." Phil had seen him too and approached the car. "If you're stopping by to see our favorite little chocolate bunny, I hate to disappoint you, but she's out to lunch with some friends."

"Who's minding the shop?" Ethan asked to cover his disappointment.

"Her assistant is decorating some candies. You should go in and see what she does to those things." Phil waved a pink and brown striped bag. "Couldn't resist buying a few."

"I'm not a big chocolate fan." Ethan had no claims on Chloe, but he wondered how often Phil visited the shop. Was a chocolate addiction the man's only reason?

"You here to talk business?" Phil opened the bag and studied his purchase. "I have a lot of clients on this block. You know how it is—I clean, they talk. I hear a lot from the merchants in this neighborhood. They've made Chloe into some kind of hero."

"A hero?" Ethan asked. Phil seemed eager to share the gossip with him.

"Yes. Most of the shop owners here are independents—they fear people like you." Phil popped a candy into his mouth, chewed, and swallowed in one motion. "Chloe may not look so tough, but she's become their hero for standing up to you."

Ethan shrugged. "I never let neighborhood gossip guide my decisions." His thoughts, however, belied his words. Chloe's style, strength, and courage were the very characteristics that he found so attractive.

Plus, while he might not be a chocolate connoisseur, in his short association with Chloe Ethan had learned a thing or two about how to eat fine chocolate, and Phil Webb was doing it all wrong.

The other thing Mr. Swifter was wrong about was Chloe's disinterest in Ethan. Sure, she'd refused his latest offer, but the way she'd looked at him the other night showed she was anything but indifferent. He needed to talk to her.

"Is Chloe expected back soon?" Ethan asked.

"She's taking the afternoon off. Shopping for a dress." Phil nodded over his shoulder at a poster in the chocolate shop window. "There's some big chocolate event next weekend."

"I heard about it," Ethan said.

Ethan waited for Phil to get into his van and drive away before he stepped out onto the curb.

"Where you going?" Brad asked.

"Into the Chocolate Boutique."

"What for?" Brad got out of the car and followed. "You just said you're not a big fan of chocolate. And Chloe's not there."

"I'm shopping for my father." His response was an outright lie. His mom was relenting, allowing his father to eat an occasional vanilla custard chocolate.

"Really." Brad put a hand on his chin. "Can't you buy the same kind of candy anywhere in the city?"

"I don't know," Ethan snapped. "My folks were specific about buying them from Chloe."

"Mom and Pop seem to be willing to tip the calorie

count in favor of their favorite chocolatier. Have they been drawn in by her magical chocolate seduction?" Brad elbowed Ethan. "What about their son?"

"Haven't you heard that dark chocolate is good for you?"

"And so is the lady who sells it." Brad chuckled.

Ethan ignored Brad, but his had words added more food for thought. Chloe was sexy, seductive, a bit kooky, and somehow magical. Ethan couldn't get her out of his mind. She had stymied his ability to think like a sharp businessman. She had become an addiction. He wasn't sure how it had happened, but except for a few close friends, she seemed to understand him better than anyone he had ever met. She had turned out to be just the kind of woman he wanted in his life.

Uh-oh. Changing his game plan in the middle of the game was never a good idea.

Chapter Fourteen

Chloe had found the perfect dress. Delicate beads dripped down the front like melted sugar. It was just a tad too long, but no problem for Sadie, who had trimmed the hem and used the remaining fabric to decorate her mask. The tenant in apartment 2B, a beauty-school student, offered to do Chloe's hair. She suggested a softer image and arranged Chloe's hair in layers around her face. Her fading pink tips would fall gently over the mask Sadie had so lovingly created.

"You were meant to wear this dress," Sadie sighed. "I wonder if the previous owner looked as stunning in it as you do."

"I'm sure she did. The salesgirl at the thrift shop

said it was a one-of-a-kind design made exclusively for some famous actress."

"Well, it's yours now, and you look beautiful. Now, off to your party." Sadie handed her a padded box with the delicate mask inside. "Mr. Liang's son didn't have a limo available this evening, so he sent a town car instead."

"It really wasn't necessary. I would have splurged and taken a cab," Chloe protested as they pushed her out the front door toward the waiting car.

It was a short ride to the museum, where Chloe would meet Date #3. Even though she had more important things to worry about, she was a little anxious over her mysterious date for the evening. She pushed the thought from her mind as the car left her at the Brooklyn Museum.

Lights flooded through the open doors to the exhibit hall. Small twinkling lanterns had been strung along the paths leading to the various displays. Masked guests circulated around the room, admiring the Mayan exhibit and decadent chocolate displays. She looked closely at the men who seemed unattached. Any of the masked men could be her date for the evening.

Earlier Chloe had arranged for her chocolate pizza to be sent by special courier. She had made an extra one and sent it to the Behars'.

Tonight, her first priority was to see that the pizza

had arrived safely. She put on her mask, careful not to twist the delicate arrangement of beads cascading down her cheeks. Across the room a woman waved at her. It would be a challenge to recognize any of her friends, so she crossed the floor for a better look.

"How ya doin?" It was easy to identify Maddie by her distinct New York accent.

Chloe listened while Maddie explained to a group of foodies how she had created her magnificent *torta di chocolate.* Maddie's description of the torte was so real, Chloe's taste buds watered. A combination of moist chocolate cake with a creamy ganache center. She would have to wait. Only the judges had been given the privilege of tasting the entries.

When Maddie finished, she turned to Chloe and asked, "Where's your date for this evening?"

Chloe twisted a napkin into a tight stick and said, "I don't know if he's even here yet."

"Didn't Sarah give you a clue? Is he going to wear a flower or something?"

"No. She said he'll recognize me." She twisted the napkin tighter, breaking it in two. "I never should have agreed to a blind date for this evening."

"If he's really repulsive, you can always dump him and get lost in the crowd." Maddie put an arm around Chloe's shoulders. "I feel for you. I've had my share of dates from hell."

"You have no idea what I've dated lately." Chloe

managed a faint nod, then smiled. Maddie would never believe she had dated a hot dog and a man who drove around under a toilet bowl brush. "Let's take your foodies over to see my pizza."

Surrounded by a gaggle of chocolate fans, Chloe was about to explain how she had made the crust when a loud, booming voice called her name.

"Hey, Chloe, there you are." A man in a hideous mask approached. There were other strange masks in the room, but none as offensive as this one.

"Who would wear a mask like that to a chocolate ball? It looks like a huge hairy bug," Maddie whispered into Chloe's ear.

"I know someone who would. A self-promoter like Phil Webb, Mr. Swifter, would take advantage of this evening to push his cleaning service."

"Does he sell bug spray? How do you know him?"

"We sort of dated." Chloe's impulse was to run and hide. Sarah couldn't be so cruel. Maybe she was giving Phil another chance because their date had been intercepted by Ethan?

Phil tilted his mask back, exposing his bright smile. "I knew I'd spot you in this crowd." He greeted her with a kiss on her cheek. Too much cologne tried to cover the smell of cleaning fluids that emanated from his pores. She shuddered when a wiry tentacle brushed her face.

"Hi, Phil." She forced a smile. *Oh, my God, Sarah had said her date would know her.*

"Now, that's a chocolate." He reached toward her pizza.

Maddie grabbed his hand. "This is a display. You can't just help yourself."

"Phil, this is my friend, Maddie. She's a chocolate chef too."

"And the guardian of this table, I see," Phil said.

"Nice to meet you too," Maddie retorted. She rolled her eyes at Chloe. Ignoring Chloe's look pleading her not to desert her, Maddie feigned an excuse that she had to check on the other entries.

Chloe couldn't blame Maddie. She wished she could vanish too.

"I know what I'd really like to taste tonight." He leaned forward and whispered into her ear. "You look absolutely delicious. Too bad Sarah said you already had a date for tonight."

"Sarah told you I had a date?" Chloe brushed the wiry tentacles from her face and almost laughed out loud. "I do." She looked around the room. "I seem to have lost him in the crowd."

"What kind a date loses someone who looks like you?" Phil twirled her around, just missing the display table.

Chloe was set off balance by the sudden move and

positioned her hands on his shoulders to steady herself. Trying to sound as convincing as possible, she said, "He'll be right back."

"I'd love to hang around to meet him, but I've got a date too. You know Emily?" He released Chloe and reached for the girl to his right. She lifted her mask. "Emily works for the hairdresser next to your shop."

"Emily, how nice to see you." Chloe didn't know if she should laugh or feel sad. Of course she was relieved that Phil had come with Emily, but now that Phil was eliminated as her date for the evening, she had no idea what to expect.

Phil grinned at Chloe over his shoulder as Emily swept him off to the dance floor. Chloe pretended to continue searching the crowd for her date. From her vantage point in the center of the hall, she had a good view of the room. Maddie had rejoined her foodie friends.

Chloe watched as the guests mingled at the entrance, then withdrew to the display tables, where they mingled again. There appeared to be a pattern to the way everyone maneuvered through the space. A subtle shift in the movement of the crowd caused Chloe to follow the glances of several women. They were watching a man who had just entered the hall.

Maddie had noticed him too. She winked at Chloe from across the room. With a thumbs-up she signaled that maybe this handsome stranger could be Chloe's date.

But the handsome man was not a stranger. Chloe's knees felt like softening taffy. She knew exactly who was under the black Venetian mask.

Dressed in an elegant custom tux, Ethan Behar surveyed the room. To her surprise, he chose the path to his right and studied the contents of the display case for a few minutes. A few steps over were some of the Mayan artifacts Chloe's parents had on loan to the museum.

Ethan had every right to be there. This was a public event open to anyone who paid the high price of the ticket. There was no question that Ethan Behar had the funds.

Chloe turned away. Minutes ticked by while she thought about how she was going to handle coming face-to-face with him. Would he be so bold as to greet her with a kiss? Of course he would, and she wouldn't object, just like she hadn't when she melted in his arms on her kitchen floor.

She turned back and looked for him in the crowd. He wasn't difficult to find. He was the most attractive man she had seen all evening, and he was walking directly toward her. There had been no contact between them since the baggy-pants accountant had shown up in her shop with that crazy offer.

She wasn't sure if Ethan had spotted her. In excruciating slow motion he took his time ambling across the room. At the edge of the dance floor a woman smiled at him from beneath her mask. He took a moment to chat with her. Chloe felt a pang of jealousy.

She reached for a chocolate martini off a passing tray, but Ethan got to it first. With a glass in each hand he came to stand in front of her.

Overwhelmed by his closeness, she managed a soft, "Hi, Ethan."

He handed her a glass but didn't speak. He seemed to be studying her, trying to penetrate her mask.

She took a sip and studied him through the slits in her mask. His mask ended just above his upper lip with a full view of his arrogant jaw and strong, masculine features. The mask itself fit like his custom-made tuxedo.

She let her eyes, half-hidden by her own mask, explore every inch of him. She could tell he was doing the same to her, and the thought ignited her entire body.

"Sarah said you would stand out in the crowd, but I had no idea you were going to look *this* good." He fingered the pearls along her cheek. "Look at you, all decked out in jewels. And your hair." The back of his hand brushed across her skin.

Oh, my god. Sarah had really gone and done it. She had arranged a date with Ethan.

Something stirred inside Chloe. Maybe it was his touch, the smell of chocolate in the air, or the security of their masks, but she wanted to play this game with Ethan.

The first step, their introduction, had been completed. She could act coy and pretend she had no idea what he was talking about, but instead she chose to be bold. Her mask gave her a sense of power.

She allowed him to thread her arm through his. Her breath quickened, but she offered no resistance as he led her onto the dance floor.

Chloe had never been comfortable dancing, but tonight was different. Ethan's hand, placed strategically on her back, guided her across the floor to a wild Latin beat. Her hips moved naturally as she followed his lead. The beads of her dress swayed in the opposite direction of her hips. It was fun and sexy. She was powerless, allowing her body to respond to the seduction of the dance. Ethan stepped forward, enticing her. She stepped away, teasing him. They repeated the movements across the entire dance floor.

When the music slowed, he pulled her close.

She looked up at the black mask and asked, "Where did you learn to dance so well?" She needed a distraction, something to take her mind off the tingling in her stomach.

"My mother is a firm believer in teaching sons to dance. She insisted we take lessons." He leaned close and whispered into her ear, "You're not so bad either."

She liked this side of Ethan, the man whose mother had made him take dance lessons. She inhaled his familiar, citrusy aftershave and surrendered to the masterful seduction of both her partner and the music.

She let the rhythm of his breathing blend with the slow Latin beat. If it was at all possible, he pulled her closer with every step. The beads of her dress rolled softly over her skin, creating a powerful sensation against her thighs. Did Ethan feel it too?

The music stopped, but Chloe hadn't noticed. Her heart still hammered in her ears. The bandleader announced, "The judges are ready to announce our chocolate recipe winners."

Nothing had been more important to Chloe than having her entry win for best chocolate recipe of the year—until now. She and Ethan stood facing each other on the dance floor, oblivious to what was going on around them.

It was Maddie who broke their trance. "C'mon, don't you want to hear the winners?" She tugged gently, pulling Chloe toward the front of the dance floor. The crowd closed in around them.

Chloe turned to look at Ethan, who signaled for her to go on without him. She and Maddie stood hand in hand and listened as the judges announced the runners-up. Neither of their entries was named. They smiled at each other and crossed their fingers. Their entries were still in the running.

Chloe held her breath as the third-place winner was announced.

"Chloe Brandeau from the Chocolate Boutique!"

Chloe squeezed Maddie's hand. "Good luck," she whispered, and she went up to the stage to receive her trophy and prize money.

Ethan stood out in the haze of masked faces. Just below the line of his mask the corners of his lips raised in a provocative smile, and Chloe felt as if she had won the grand prize.

Maddie did not take second place, and Chloe felt a bit anxious that her friend was out of the running. A loud fanfare preceded the announcement of the grand prize winner.

"Maddie Higgins and her wonderful signature dessert, a perfect *Torta di Chocolate*, is our Grand Prize winner!"

Chloe remembered the year she and Max had won the grand prize. She congratulated Maddie and stepped off the stage, where Ethan and other well-wishers waited to congratulate her. Ethan, however, slipped to the back of the crowd, allowing her colleagues to close in around her.

Chloe was surprised when her cousin, Allen, stepped forward. "Good job, Chloe. My mother would be proud."

"Allen, what are you doing here?"

"My daughter, Carrie, has taken an interest in chocolate making. She had an extra ticket and dragged me along."

The crowd moved on to congratulate Maddie and the other winners. Allen ushered Chloe to an empty table. A waiter passed with samples of the entries, and Allen reached for one.

"I noticed you earlier. You were with Ethan Behar."

"You recognized him even with his mask?"

"The mask looked like it had been custom-made for his face. And his face is very recognizable since this Butler Street project started." Allen took a sample of Chloe's pizza. "You wouldn't happen to know why he called my office last week, would you? I thought it might have something to do with the Butler Street building."

"I'm sure you're right about that." Chloe tried to hide her resentment. The night had been perfect, and she didn't want anything to ruin it, but Allen's mention of Ethan and her apartment building in the same sentence brought back the question of Ethan's motives.

"You know, at first I took offense with my mother for leaving the building to you."

"I'm sorry."

Allen held up his hands. "Don't apologize. Mom— Aunt—Bessie made the right choice. I would have sold the building by now and put my mother's friends out on the street. You're kind of a hero in the neighborhood."

"I am?"

"Sure. I hear it all the time from my clients how you're standing up to Ethan Behar and what he represents." He cleared his throat. "I'm a little surprised to see the two of you together here."

"Oh, it's not what you think. I mean, I'm not selling to him and would never let anyone leave my tenants homeless, so tonight is not what you think."

"However you're doing it, keep up the good work." He turned to leave but then had something to add. "Did you ever think we were born to the wrong sisters?"

"I'm not sure what you mean."

"You seemed to have inherited my mother's knack for chocolate and making everyone around you happy." He shrugged. "On the other hand, I think digging in the dirt for old relics is really cool."

"Thanks, Allen. That was really nice of you to say."

"We're still family, and if you need any help with contracts or permits for that old building, give me a call."

After her enlightening chat with her cousin, Chloe decided to leave. She had come on her own and would go home with her trophy and prize money.

At the door Ethan appeared. "Where are you going?"

"Home."

"Let me get my car."

"No, thanks. I'll take the subway."

"The subway?" He glanced at his watch. "It's almost midnight."

She kept walking, down the steps and onto the sidewalk.

"What's wrong?" He increased his pace to catch up to her.

"Why did you call my cousin?" Chloe removed her mask. Other guests were waiting for their cars. The party was breaking up.

"How do you know about that?" Ethan moved her off to one side, out of earshot of the departing guests.

"Don't answer my question with a question."

Ethan ran a finger along her shoulder. "Things have changed since I made that call."

She played with the ribbon on her mask. Anything to help her ignore the overwhelming pleasure of his touch. "Oh, really. Like what?"

"You can't pretend that tonight was just a game."

She looked at him and wanted to argue that it had started out as a game on her part, but being in his arms had changed the game plan. "You still want my building?"

"Chloe, let's not confuse the issues."

"The issue is, I'm not sure if you want me more than you want my building," she almost screamed. "You may be a master of acquisitions, but you sure have a lot to learn about relationships." She turned and started to walk away, then stopped and added one more comment. "And don't try to pretend that you like chocolate."

The briskness of her turn caused a line of beads to catch on an iron. The sly smile on Ethan's face annoyed her even more, but she had no place to go. A sudden movement could unravel the front of her dress.

He walked slowly toward her. "Don't move."

She was at his mercy. Biting her upper lip, she refrained from saying something she might regret.

With surprising dexterity Ethan's fingers unraveled the thread.

Light from a streetlamp made the dress shimmer with sparks of color. She watched him roll a bead between his thumb and forefinger.

"No damage done." He looked up at her and smiled.

Heat rippled under her skin as the strand of beads fell gently back into place. Her emotions swirled, finally settling down to a slow simmer.

"Thank you." She hugged her trophy close and headed down the block alone.

Halfway down the street she heard a horn honk. She half hoped it was Ethan. The trophy was heavy, and she wasn't sure where the subway stop was.

She was disappointed when she saw the big toilet-bowl-brush van at the curb.

Phil rolled down the window. "You gonna lug that thing all the way back to Butler Street? Hop in."

With no sign of Ethan's SUV, she had no other option. Squished in the front seat with Phil and his date, she held the trophy in her lap.

Luckily the ride was short. When they pulled up in front of her building, Sadie was walking her bulldog puppy. There was nothing unusual about seeing Sadie walking her puppy after midnight. What was weird, however, was the presence of the other tenants on the street. Had they all been waiting for Chloe to return? That seemed unlikely.

She glanced at the façade of her building. Everything seemed to be intact. She stepped from the van, and everyone rushed forward at once, jabbering in fragmented sentences about a busted pipe and two inches of water on the floor. Where were they to go?

No one commented on her trophy or how nice she looked. Chloe thanked Phil and proceeded toward the front door.

"No, don't open the door," several voices warned.

Too late. Chloe's heart sank deep into her stomach. At least an inch of water greeted her when she pushed open the door to the lobby.

Behind her Mr. Liang said, "It seems like a big pipe this time."

Chloe took off her shoes and stepped into the lobby. Music drifted from an open door, a sexy Latin beat. For a moment she was back in Ethan's arms, teasing and being teased as they moved across the dance floor.

She glanced over her shoulder at the desperate faces waiting for her to say something. Reality hit her full force.

Chapter Fifteen

One too many inspectors showed up the next morning. If Chloe wanted them to vanish, she knew that one call to Ethan would make them disappear, but that wasn't her plan.

After being served with a list of violations that were supposedly jeopardizing the safety of her tenants, she called a tenants' meeting and discussed the options with everyone. Led by Sadie and Mr. Liang, the tenants all agreed to stay in their apartments until they were forced to move. And they would most likely have to be forced.

Chloe wasn't going to let it come to that. Fortunately, the building was not condemned, and she had been given a two-month allowance to correct the vio-

176

lations. An early-morning visit from Henry had easily corrected several of the minor problems. A water-restoration crew had responded last night, and this morning the hallways were dry.

First thing in the morning she called Cousin Allen and discussed her idea. If Ethan agreed to let her tenants stay until they chose to leave, she would agree to sell Ethan a share of her building. But Chloe must be allowed to remain the major shareholder. The money she received would be used to make major repairs. Ethan would be allowed to redesign the exterior with setbacks to fit the plan for his Butler Street project. As apartments became vacant, he would be allowed to renovate, but only after all living relatives of the previous tenant relinquished their rights to the apartment. And, most important, she would have the final say on any rent increases.

Even though it was Sunday, Allen promised to have the contracts ready so Ethan could review them before the meeting he had scheduled for later that day. Everything would be just the way Ethan liked it—all business and no pleasure. She wouldn't even offer him chocolate.

She opened her shop, confident that everything would work out.

Traffic in and out of the shop was heavy for a Sunday morning. Business would be good after her third-place win was announced in the local papers. The onslaught of orders was, of cause, just a phase that would pass with the next chocolate craze, but she and Maddie planned to take advantage of their newly elevated status.

On her way to the city, Maddie stopped by with a tray of her *torta di chocolate.*

"I thought I'd see Ethan Behar here. You two seemed to hit it off great last night."

"Date number three didn't turn out to be any more successful than the other two." Chloe wasn't about to let the mention of Ethan drag her down.

"You two sure had me fooled. You should have seen the way he looked at you when you weren't with him." Maddie gave her curious glance. "What is it you don't like about him?"

"Maddie, don't you have to get to your restaurant?" She placed Maddie's dessert in a prime location and steered her friend toward the door.

Before Maddie could leave, Sarah and Henry came rushing in.

"Oh, my god. Henry told me what happened last night." Sarah rushed forward and hugged Chloe. "Not another flood. Was it really as bad as everyone is saying?"

"It wasn't a very pleasant way to end my evening, but everything is under control." Chloe kneaded her shoulder, working out a kink.

"Too much dancing?" Sarah asked. She looked

around the shop. "I thought Ethan would be here this morning."

Chloe looked at her friends. "Why does everyone expect Ethan to be here?"

"I don't know. I thought maybe after last night the two of you would . . ." Sarah pulled out a chair and waited for someone to tell her what had happened at the ball.

Chloe had no intention of spending her morning discussing Ethan Behar. The best way to put an end to everyone's curiosity was to tell them what they wanted to hear and send them on their way.

"Ethan and I enjoyed a few dances, and then business got in the way."

"It did?" Sarah asked, but she looked at Maddie for confirmation.

Maddie shrugged. "It looked like it was going to be more than just a few dances, if you ask me. I saw them leave together."

So that was it. Everyone was under the impression that Chloe's evening with Ethan hadn't ended when the ball was over. "Actually, Phil Webb drove me home."

"Phil?" everyone said in unison.

"Yes, Mr. Swifter, in his truck with the toilet-bowl brush on top. He and his date were kind enough to drive me and my trophy home." Chloe tried to concentrate on her friends' surprised expressions. "You know the rest. I had other issues to deal with when I got home." The truth was, the flood had given her something other than Ethan to think about.

When everyone finally left, Chloe got down to the business of selling candy. The afternoon passed without any more inquiries into her evening. The only mention of the ball came from well-wishers and customers interested in her chocolate.

There were several customers in the shop when Allen arrived with the contracts. He had a cup of hot cocoa and waited for her to close up before reviewing his suggestions.

"I spoke to Ethan, and he said he would be here by closing time." Allen checked his watch. "You sure this is the way you want to go?"

"Did he say anything?" *About me?* Chloe wanted to add. She sat down and poured herself a cup of cocoa. She let the velvety texture and taste permeate her senses before she swallowed. The chocolate had the calming effect she'd hoped for.

"He's looking forward to this meeting." Allen tapped his spoon on the table. "I was surprised at how approachable he is. He was adamant that you wait for him if he's late."

"Ethan Behar, late? I doubt it."

Allen looked at his watch again. "Well, it is six, and he's not here yet."

"He'll be here." Chloe walked toward the store window. "He always makes a grand entrance."

At the window she froze. Staring back at her was a giant chocolate kiss: silver metallic fabric six feet high and six feet wide.

"That can't be Henry," she said out loud. "He's having dinner with Sarah." She stepped outside. No, it definitely wasn't Henry. The giant kiss wore designer Italian shoes, and the creases in his black pants were impeccably pressed.

"Ethan?"

"Your cousin said to be here at six sharp." The voice, deep and masculine, sent a familiar flutter through her. "Sorry I'm a few minutes late, but this thing is a pain to get into."

He had no idea how his voice affected her. She peered at the mesh eyes cut into the costume. She wished she could see his face. Could he see hers? Did he see her smiling?

"What are you doing in that ridiculous thing?" She laughed.

"Trying to be better at relationships. And to prove I really do like chocolate."

"I didn't ask you to come here to confess your inadequacies. I have a deal to discuss with you."

"I looked over the papers your cousin, Allen, faxed earlier. I think it's a great idea for us to be partners."

"You do?" Chloe couldn't believe she was standing there talking to Ethan dressed as a giant chocolate kiss.

"Yes, I want our life together to be a wonderful partnership. Keep your building. I'll give you the entire block if you want it."

"What would I do with an entire block?" Chloe wanted to make sure she understood what he was saying. "Would you really sacrifice your project for me?"

"There'll be other projects, but I doubt there's another you."

Chloe felt as if her heart was going to beat out of her chest. Nothing ever went the way she planned when Ethan showed up, but this time she didn't mind one morsel.

"Hey, you still out there?"

She managed a nod, unsure if her voice would clear her throat.

"Help me out of this thing." He turned around and, with huge, white-gloved hands, pointed to the zipper.

She hesitated. "You know chocolate is my weakness." She giggled as Ethan stepped out of his costume. "I don't know if I'll have the power to resist you."

"I'm hoping you can't."

She threw her arms around his neck. "I'm finding it very difficult."

"Chloe, I can't resist *you*. From the first day I showed

up here, I haven't been able to stay away. I think I pursued this deal because I was afraid if I gave up, I would never see you again." He slipped his arms around her. "Tell me that you want me to stick around. Give me a chance to show you that I care more about you than any deal."

Across the street Brad put his hand on the horn of the SUV. Allen stepped out of the shop, glanced in their direction, ripped the contract in half, and tossed it into the trash.

Chloe, oblivious to the sounds around her, leaned closer and whispered, "Where do you want me to sign?"

Ethan laughed. "I've got a better way to seal this deal." He kissed her gently on the lips.

"If I had known your deal-closing technique was so persuasive, I might have signed sooner." She returned his kiss with one sweeter than her most intoxicating chocolate.